The Collector's Wodehouse

P. G. WODEHOUSE

A Few Quick Ones

THE OVERLOOK PRESS
WOODSTOCK & NEW YORK

This edition first published in the United States in 2009 by
The Overlook Press, Peter Mayer Publishers, Inc.
Woodstock and New York

WOODSTOCK
One Overlook Drive
Woodstock, NY 12498
www.overlookpress.com
[for individual orders, bulk and special sales, contact our Woodstock office]

NEW YORK
141 Wooster Street
New York, NY 10012

First published by Simon and Schuster, New York, 1959
Copyright © 1948, 1958, 1959 by P. G. Wodehouse
Some of the stories in this collection previously published in *Playboy*, *Collier's*,
Lilliput, *This Week* and *John Bull*
© 1947 by Hearst Magazine, Inc © 1953 by Crowell-Collier Publishing Co.
© 1954 by The McCall Corporation © 1958 by HMH Publishing Company, Inc.
© 1958 by United Newspaper Magazine Corp.

Cataloging-in-Publication Data is available from the Library of Congress

Manufactured in Germany

ISBN 978-1-59020-241-8

1 3 5 7 9 8 6 4 2

moment he is rather unfortunately situated. He owes a bookie fifty quid, and is temporarily unable to settle.'

'Silly ass.'

'Silly, unquestionably, ass, but there it is. What happened was that he drew an uncle in this sweep whom nobody had ever heard of, and blow me tight if he hadn't unexpectedly hit the jackpot. He showed me a snapshot of the man, and I was amazed. I could see at a glance that here was the winner, so far ahead of the field that there could be no competition. Blicester would be an honourable runner-up, but nothing more. Extraordinary how often in these big events you find a dark horse popping up and upsetting all calculations. Well, with the sweepstake money as good as in his pocket, as you might say, poor old Freddie lost his head and put his shirt on a horse at Kempton Park which finished fourth, with the result, as I have indicated, that he owes this bookie fifty quid, and no means of paying him till he collects on the sweep. And the bookie, when informed that he wasn't going to collect, advised him in a fatherly way to be very careful of himself from now on, for though he knew that it was silly to be superstitious, he – the bookie – couldn't help remembering that every time people did him down for money some unpleasant accident always happened to them. Time after time he had noticed it, and it could not be mere coincidence. More like some sort of fate, the bookie said. So Freddie is lying low, disguised in a beard by Clarkson.'

'Where?'

'In East Dulwich.'

'Whereabouts in East Dulwich?'

'Ah,' said the Egg, 'that's what the bookie would like to know.'

The trouble about East Dulwich, from the point of view of a cleanshaven man trying to find a bearded man there, is that it is rather densely populated, rendering his chances of success slim. Right up to the day before the Eton and Harrow match Oofy prowled to and fro in its streets, hoping for the best, but East Dulwich held its secret well. The opening day of the match found him on the steps of the Drones Club, scanning the horizon like Sister Anne in the Bluebeard story. Surely, he felt, Freddie could not stay away from the premises on this morning of mornings.

Member after member entered the building as he stood there, accompanied by uncles of varying stoutness, but not one of those members was Freddie Widgeon, and Oofy's blood pressure had just reached a new high and looked like going to par, when a cab drew up and something bearded, shooting from its interior, shot past him, shot through the entrance hall and disappeared down the steps leading to the washroom. The eleventh hour had produced the man.

Freddie, when Oofy burst into the washroom some moments later with a 'Tally-ho' on his lips, was staring at himself in the mirror, a thing not many would have cared to do when looking as he did. A weaker man than Oofy would have recoiled at the frightful sight that met his eyes. Freddie, when making his purchase at Clarkson's, had evidently preferred quantity to quality. The salesman, no doubt, had recommended something in neat Vandykes as worn by the better class of ambassadors, but Freddie was a hunted stag, and when hunted stags buy beards, they want something big and bushy as worn by Victorian novelists. The man whom Oofy had been seeking so long could at this moment of their meeting have stepped into the Garrick Club of the Sixties, and Wilkie Collins and the rest of the boys would have welcomed him as a brother, supposing him to be Walt Whitman.

'Freddie!' cried Oofy.

'Oh, hullo, Oofy,' said Freddie. He was pulling at the beard in a gingerly manner, as if the process hurt him. 'You are doubtless surprised—'

'No, I'm not. I was warned of this. Why don't you take that damned thing off?'

'I can't.'

'Give it a tug.'

'I have given it a tug, and the agony was excruciating. It's stuck on with spirit gum or something.'

'Well, never mind your beard. We have no time to talk of beards. Freddie, thank heaven I have found you. Another quarter of an hour, and it would have been too late.'

'What would have been too late?'

'It. We've got to change those tickets.'

'What, again?'

'Immediately. You remember me saying that my Uncle Horace was staying at a place called Hollrock Manor in Hertfordshire? Well, naturally I supposed that it was one of those luxury country hotels where he would be having twice of everything and filling up with beer, champagne, liqueurs and what not. But was it?'

'Wasn't it? What was it if it wasn't?'

'It was what they call a clinic, run by some foul doctor, where the superfatted go to reduce. He had gone there to please a woman who had told him he looked like a hippopotamus.'

'He does look rather like a hippopotamus.'

'He does in that snapshot, I grant you, but that was taken weeks and weeks ago, and during those weeks he has been living on apple juice, tomato juice, orange juice, pineapple juice, parsnip juice, grated carrots, potassium broth and seaweed soup.

He has also been having daily massage, the term massage embracing *effleurage*, stroking, kneading, *pétrissage*, *tapotement* and vibration.'

'Lord love a duck!'

'Lord love a duck is right. I needn't tell you what happens when that sort of thing is going on. Something has to give. By now he must have lost at least a couple of stone and be utterly incapable of giving old Blicester a race. So slip me the Uncle Horace ticket, and I will slip you the Blicester, and the situation will be stabilized once more. Gosh, Freddie, old man, when I think how near I came to letting you down, thinking I was acting in your best interests, I shudder.'

Freddie stroked his beard. To Oofy's dismay, he seemed hesitant, dubious.

'Well, I'm not so sure about this,' he said. 'You say your Uncle Horace has lost a couple of stone. I am strongly of the opinion that he could lose three and still be fatter than my Uncle Rodney, and I'm wondering if I ought to take a chance. You see, a great deal hangs on my winning this tourney. I owe fifty quid to a clairvoyant bookie, who, looking in his crystal ball, has predicted that if I don't brass up, some nasty accident will happen to me, and from what he tells me that crystal ball of his is to be relied on. I should feel an awful ass if I gave up the Uncle Horace ticket and took the Uncle Rodney ticket and Uncle Horace won and I found myself in a hospital with surgeons doing crochet work all over me.'

'I only want to help.'

'I know you do, but the question is, are you helping?'

Oofy was unable to stroke his beard, for he had not got one, but he fingered his chin. He was thinking with the rapidity with which he always thought when there was money floating around to be picked up. It did not take him long to reach a decision. Agony though it was to part with fifty pounds, winning the sweep would leave him with a nice profit. There was nothing for it but to make the great sacrifice. If you do not speculate, you cannot accumulate.

'I'll tell you what I'll do,' he said, producing his wallet and extracting the bank notes with which it always bulged. 'I'll give you fifty quid. That will take care of the bookie, and you'll be all right, whatever happens.'

As much as was visible of Freddie's face between the crevices of the beard lit up. He looked like someone staring incredulously at someone through a haystack.

'Golly, Oofy! Will you really do that?'

'It's not much to do for an old friend.'

'But what is there in it for you?'

'Just that glow, old man, just that glow,' said Oofy.

Going upstairs, he found the Crumpet in the hall, studying the list in his notebook, and broke the news that a little further pencil-work would be required of him. It brought a frown to the other's face.

'I disapprove of all this chopping and changing,' he said, though agreeing that there was nothing in the rules against it. 'Let's get this straight. Freddie Widgeon now has the Blicester ticket and you have the Horace Prosser ticket. Right?'

'Yes, that's right.'

'Not vice versa?'

'No, not vice versa.'

'Good. I'm glad that's settled. I've worn out one piece of india-rubber already.'

It was at this moment that the hall porter, who for some little time had been trying to attract Oofy's attention, spoke.

'There's a gentleman asking for you, Mr Prosser. Name of Prosser, same as yours.'

'Ah, yes, my uncle. Where is he?'

'He stepped into the bar.'

'He would. Will you go and give him a cocktail,' said Oofy to the Crumpet. 'I'll be with you in a minute, after I've booked a table in the dining-room.'

It was with the feeling that all was for the best in this best of all possible worlds that he entered the dining-room. Like the Battle of Waterloo, it had been a devilish close-run thing, but he had won through, and his morale was high. He did not actually say 'Tra-la' as he ordered his table, but the ejaculation was implicit in the sunniness of his smile and the sparkle in his eyes. Coming out again into the hall with a gay air on his lips, he was surprised to find the Crumpet there.

'Hullo,' he said. 'Didn't you go to the bar?'

'I went.'

'Didn't you find the old boy?'

'I found him.' The Crumpet's manner seemed strange to Oofy. He was looking grave and reproachful, like a Crumpet who considers that he has been played fast and loose with. 'Oofy,' he said, 'fun's fun, and no one's fonder of a joke than I am, but there are limits. I can see no excuse for a fellow pulling a gag in connection with a race meeting as important as this one. You knew the rules governing the sweep perfectly well. Only genuine uncles were eligible. I suppose you thought it would be humorous to ring in a non-uncle.'

'Do what?'

'It's as bad as entering a greyhound for the Grand National.'

Oofy could make nothing of this. The thought flitted through his mind that the other had been lunching.

'What on earth are you talking about?'

'I'm talking about that bloke in there with the billowy curves. You said he was your uncle.'

'He is my uncle.'

'He is nothing of the bally sort.'

'His name's Prosser.'

'No doubt.'

'He signed his letter "Uncle Horace".'

'Very possibly. But that doesn't alter the stark fact that he's a sort of distant cousin. He was telling me about it while we quaffed. It appears that as a child you used to call him Uncle Horace but, stripped of his mask, he is, as I say, merely a distant cousin. If you didn't know this and were not just trying to be funny when you entered him, I apologize for my recent remarks. You are more to be pitied than censured, it would seem, for the blighter is of course disqualified and the stakes go to Frederick Fortescue Widgeon, holder of the Blicester ticket.'

To think simultaneously of what might have been and what is going to be is not an easy task, but Oofy, as he heard these words of doom, found himself doing it. For even as his mind dwelled on the thought that he had paid Freddie Widgeon fifty pounds to deprive himself of the sweepstake money, he was also vividly aware that in a brace of shakes he would be standing his distant cousin Horace a lunch which, Horace being the man he was, could scarcely put him in the hole for less than a fiver. His whole soul seethed like a cistern struck by a thunderbolt, and everything seemed to go black.

The Crumpet was regarding him with concern.

'Don't gulp like that, Oofy,' he said. 'You can't be sick here.'

Oofy was not so sure. He was feeling as if he could be sick anywhere.

A devout expression had come into the face of the young man in plus fours who sat with the Oldest Member on the terrace overlooking the ninth green. With something of the abruptness of a conjurer taking a rabbit out of a hat he drew a photograph from his left breast pocket and handed it to his companion. The Sage inspected it thoughtfully.

'This is the girl you were speaking of?'

'Yes.'

'You love her?'

'Madly.'

'And how do you find it affects your game?'

'I've started shanking a bit.'

The Oldest Member nodded.

'I am sorry,' he said, 'but not surprised. Either that or missing short putts is what generally happens on these occasions. I doubt if golfers ought to fall in love. I have known it to cost men ten shots in a medal round. They think of the girl and forget to keep their eyes on the ball. On the other hand, there was the case of Harold Pickering.'

'I don't think I've met him.'

'He was before your time. He took a cottage here a few years ago. His handicap was fourteen. Yet within a month of his arrival love had brought him down to scratch.'

'Quick service.'

'Very. He went back eventually to a shaky ten, but the fact remains. But for his great love he would not have become even temporarily a scratch man.'

I had seen Harold Pickering in and about the clubhouse (said the Oldest Member) for some time before I made his acquaintance, and there was something in his manner which suggested that sooner or later he would be seeking me out and telling me the story of his life. For some reason, possibly because I have white whiskers, I seem to act on men with stories of their lives to tell like catnip on cats. And sure enough, I was sitting on this terrace one evening, enjoying a quiet gin-and-ginger, when he sidled up, coughed once or twice like a sheep with bronchitis and gave me the works.

His was a curious and romantic tale. He was by profession a partner in a publishing house, and shortly before his arrival here he had gone to negotiate with John Rockett for the purchase of his Reminiscences.

The name John Rockett will, of course, be familiar to you. If you are a student of history, you will recall that he was twice British Amateur Champion and three times runner-up in the Open. He had long retired from competition golf and settled down to a life of leisured ease, and when Harold Pickering presented himself he found the great veteran celebrating his silver wedding. All the family were there – his grandmother, now ageing a little but in her day a demon with the gutty ball; his wife, at one time British Ladies Champion; his three sons, Sandwich, Hoylake and St Andrew; and his two daughters, Troon and Prestwick. He called his children after the courses on which he had won renown, and they did not disgrace the honoured names. They were all scratch.

In a gathering so august, you might have supposed that a sense of what was fitting would have kept a fourteen-handicap man from getting above himself. But passion knows no class distinctions. Ten minutes after his arrival, Harold Pickering had fallen in love with Troon Rockett, with a fervour which could not have been more wholehearted if he had been playing to plus two. And a week later he put his fortune to the test, to win or lose it all.

'Of course, I was mad ... mad,' he said, moodily chewing the ham sandwich he had ordered, for he had had only a light lunch. 'How could I suppose that a girl who was scratch – the sister of scratch men – the daughter of an amateur champion – would stoop to a fellow like me? Even as I started to speak, I saw the horror and amazement on her face. Well, when I say speak, I didn't exactly speak, I sort of gargled. But it was enough. She rose quickly and left the room. And I came here—'

'To forget her?'

'Talk sense,' said Harold Pickering shortly. 'I came to try to make myself worthy of her. I intended to get myself down to scratch, if it choked me. I heard that your pro here was the best instructor in the country, so I signed the lease for a cottage, seized my clubs and raced round to his shop ... only to discover what?'

'That he has broken his leg?'

'Exactly. What a sensible, level-headed pro wants to break his leg for is more than I can imagine. But there it was. No chance of any lessons from him.'

'It must have been a shock for you.'

'I was stunned. It seemed to me that this was the end. But now things have brightened considerably. Do you know a Miss Flack?'

I did indeed. Agnes Flack was one of the recognized sights of the place. One pointed her out to visitors together with the

Lovers Leap, the waterfall and the curious rock formation near the twelfth tee. Built rather on the lines of the village blacksmith, she had for many seasons been the undisputed female champion of the club. She had the shoulders of an all-in wrestler, the breezy self-confidence of a sergeant-major and a voice like a toastmaster's. I had often seen the Wrecking Crew, that quartette of spavined septuagenarians whose pride it was that they never let anyone through, scatter like leaves in an autumn gale at the sound of her stentorian 'Fore!' A dynamic and interesting personality.

'She is going to coach me,' said Harold Pickering. 'I saw her practising chip shots my first morning here, and I was amazed at her virtuosity. She seemed just to give a flick of the wrist and the ball fell a foot from the pin and flopped there like a poached egg. It struck me immediately that here was someone whose methods I could study to my great advantage. The chip is my weak spot. For the last ten days or so, accordingly, I have been following her about the course, watching her every movement, and yesterday we happened to fall into conversation and I confided my ambition to her. With a hearty laugh, she told me that if I wanted to become scratch I had come to the right shop. She said that she could make a scratch player out of a cheese mite, provided it had not lost the use of its limbs, and gave as evidence of her tuitionary skill the fact that she had turned a man named Sidney McMurdo from a mere blot on the local scene into something which in a dim light might be mistaken for a golfer. I haven't met McMurdo.'

'He is away at the moment. He has gone to attend the sickbed of an uncle. He will be back to play for the club championship.'

'As hot as that, is he?'

'Yes, I suppose he would be about the best man we have.'

'Scratch?'

'Plus one, I believe, actually.'

'And what was he before Miss Flack took him in hand?'

'His handicap, if I remember rightly, was fifteen.'

'You don't say?' said Harold Pickering, his face lighting up. 'Was it, by Jove? Then this begins to look like something. If she could turn him into such a tiger, there's a chance for me. We start the lessons tomorrow.'

I did not see Harold Pickering for some little time after this, an attack of lumbago confining me to my bed, but stories of his prowess filtered through to my sickroom, and from these it was abundantly evident that his confidence in Agnes Flack's skill as an instructress had not been misplaced. He won a minor competition with such ease that his handicap was instantly reduced to eight. Then he turned in a series of cards which brought him down to four. And the first thing I saw on entering the clubhouse on my restoration to health was his name on the list of entrants for the club championship. Against it was the word 'scratch'.

I can remember few things that have pleased me more. We are all sentimentalists at heart, and the boy's story had touched me deeply. I hastened to seek him out and congratulate him. I found him practising approach putts on the ninth green, but when I gripped his hand it was like squeezing a wet fish. His whole manner was that of one who has not quite shaken off the effects of being struck on the back of the head by a thunderbolt. It surprised me for a moment, but then I remembered that the achievement of a great ambition often causes a man to feel for a while somewhat filleted. The historian Gibbon, if you recall, had that experience on finishing his Decline and Fall of the Roman Empire, and I saw the same thing once in a friend of mine who had just won a Littlewood's pool.

'Well,' I said cheerily, 'I suppose you will now be leaving us? You will want to hurry off to Miss Rockett with the great news.'

He winced and topped a putt.

'No,' he said, 'I'm staying on here. My fiancée seems to wish it.'

'Your fiancée?'

'I am engaged to Agnes Flack.'

I was astounded. I had always understood that Agnes Flack was betrothed to Sidney McMurdo. I was also more than a little shocked. It was only a few weeks since he had poured out his soul to me on the subject of Troon Rockett, and this abrupt switching of his affections to another seemed to argue a sad lack of character and stability. When young fellows are enamoured of a member of the other sex, I like them to stay enamoured.

'Well, I hope you will be very happy,' I said.

'You needn't try to be funny,' he rejoined bitterly.

There was a sombre light in his eyes, and he foozled another putt.

'The whole thing,' he said, 'is due to one of those unfortunate misunderstandings. When they made me scratch, my first move was to thank Miss Flack warmly for all she had done for me.'

'Naturally.'

'I let myself go rather.'

'You would, of course.'

'Then, feeling that after all the trouble she had taken to raise me to the heights she was entitled to be let in on the inside story, I told her my reason for being so anxious to get down to scratch was that I loved a scratch girl and wanted to be worthy of her. Upon which, chuckling like a train going through a tunnel, she gave me a slap on the back which nearly drove my spine through the front of my pullover and said she had guessed it from the very start, from the moment when she first saw me dogging her footsteps with that look of dumb devotion in my eyes. You could have knocked me down with a putter.'

'She then said she would marry you?'

'Yes. And what could I do? A girl,' said Harold Pickering fretfully, 'who can't distinguish between the way a man looks when he's admiring a chip shot thirty feet from the green and the way he looks when he's in love ought not to be allowed at large.'

There seemed nothing to say. The idea of suggesting that he should break off the engagement presented itself to me, but I dismissed it. Women are divided broadly into two classes – those who, when jilted, merely drop a silent tear and those who take a niblick from their bag and chase the faithless swain across country with it. It was to this latter section that Agnes Flack belonged. Attila the Hun might have broken off his engagement to her, but nobody except Attila the Hun, and he only on one of his best mornings.

So I said nothing, and presently Harold Pickering resumed his moody putting and I left him.

The contest for the club championship opened unsensationally. There are never very many entrants for this of course non-handicap event, and this year there were only four. Harold Pickering won his match against Rupert Watchett comfortably, and Sidney McMurdo, who had returned on the previous night, had no difficulty in disposing of George Bunting. The final, Pickering versus McMurdo, was to be played in the afternoon.

Agnes Flack had walked round with Harold Pickering in the morning, and they lunched together after the game. But an appointment with her lawyer in the metropolis made it impossible for her to stay and watch the final, and she had to be content with giving him some parting words of advice.

'The great thing,' she said, as he accompanied her to her car, 'is not to lose your nerve. Forget that it's a final and play your ordinary game, and you can trim the pants off him. This statement carries my personal guarantee.'

'You know his game pretty well?'

'Backwards. We used to do our three rounds a day together, when we were engaged.'

'Engaged?'

'Yes. Didn't I tell you? We were heading straight for the altar, apparently with no bunkers in sight, when one afternoon he took a Number Three iron when I had told him to take a Number Four. I scratched the fixture immediately. "No man," I said to him, "is going to walk up the aisle with me who takes a Number Three iron for a Number Four iron shot. Pop off, Sidney McMurdo," I said, and he gnashed his teeth and popped. I shall get the laugh of a lifetime, seeing his face when I tell him I'm engaged to you. The big lummox.'

Harold Pickering started.

'Did you say *big* lummox?'

'That was the expression I used.'

'He is robust, then?'

'Oh, he's robust enough. He could fell an ox with a single blow, if he wasn't fond of oxen.'

'And is he – er – at all inclined to be jealous?'

'Othello took his correspondence course.'

'I see,' said Harold Pickering. 'I see.'

He fell into a reverie, from which he was aroused a moment later by a deafening bellow from his companion.

'Hey, Sidney!'

The person she addressed was in Harold Pickering's rear. He turned, and perceived a vast man who gazed yearningly at Agnes Flack from beneath beetling eyebrows.

'Sidney,' said Agnes Flack, 'I want you to meet Mr Pickering, who is playing you in the final this afternoon. Mr McMurdo, Mr Pickering, my fiancé. Well, goodbye, Harold darling, I've got to rush.'

She folded him in a long lingering embrace, the car bowled off, and Harold Pickering found himself alone with this over-sized plugugly in what seemed to his fevered fancy a great empty space, like one of those ones in the movies where two strong men stand face to face and Might is the only law.

Sidney McMurdo was staring at him with a peculiar intensity. There was a disturbing gleam in his eyes, and his hands, each the size of a largish ham, were clenching and unclenching as if flexing themselves for some grim work in the not too distant future.

'Did she,' he asked in an odd, hoarse voice, 'say – fiancé?'

'Why, yes,' said Harold Pickering, with a nonchalance which it cost him a strong effort to assume. 'Yes, that's right, I believe she did.'

'You are going to marry Agnes Flack?'

'There is some idea of it, I understand.'

'Ah!' said Sidney McMurdo, and the intensity of his stare was now more marked than ever.

Harold Pickering quailed beneath it. His heart, as he gazed at this patently steamed-up colossus, missed not one beat but several. Nor, I think, can we blame him. All publishers are sensitive, highly strung men. Gollancz is. So is Hamish Hamilton. So are Chapman and Hall, Heinemann and Herbert Jenkins, Ltd. And even when in sunny mood, Sidney McMurdo was always a rather intimidating spectacle. Tall, broad, deep-chested and superbly muscled, he looked like the worthy descendant of a long line of heavyweight gorillas, and nervous people and invalids were generally warned if there was any likelihood of their meeting him unexpectedly. Harold Pickering could not but feel that an uncle who would want anything like that at his sickbed must be eccentric to the last degree.

However, he did his best to keep the conversation on a note of easy cordiality.

'Nice weather,' he said.

'Bah!' said Sidney McMurdo.

'How's your uncle?'

'Never mind my uncle. Are you busy at the moment, Mr Pickering?'

'No.'

'Good,' said Sidney McMurdo. 'Because I want to break your neck.'

There was a pause. Harold Pickering backed a step. Sidney McMurdo advanced a step. Harold Pickering backed another step. Sidney McMurdo advanced again. Harold Pickering sprang sideways. Sidney McMurdo also sprang sideways. If it had not been for the fact that the latter was gnashing his teeth and filling the air with a sound similar to that produced by an inexperienced Spanish dancer learning to play the castanets, one might have supposed them to be practising the opening movements of some graceful, old-world gavotte.

'Or, rather,' said Sidney McMurdo, correcting his previous statement, 'tear you limb from limb.'

'Why?' asked Harold Pickering, who liked to go into things.

'You know why,' said Sidney McMurdo, moving eastwards as his vis-à-vis moved westwards. 'Because you steal girls' hearts behind people's backs, like a snake.'

Harold Pickering, who happened to know something about snakes, might have challenged this description of their habits, but he was afforded no opportunity of doing so. His companion had suddenly reached out a clutching hand, and only by coyly drawing it back was he enabled to preserve his neck intact.

'Here, just a moment,' he said.

I have mentioned that publishers are sensitive and highly strung. They are also quickwitted. They think on their feet. Harold Pickering had done so now. Hodder and Stoughton could not have reacted more nimbly.

'You are proposing to tear me limb from limb, are you?'

'And also to dance on the fragments.'

It was not easy for Harold Pickering to sneer, for his lower jaw kept dropping, but he contrived to do so.

'I see,' he said, just managing to curl his lip before the jaw got away from him again. 'Thus ensuring that you shall be this year's club champion. Ingenious, McMurdo. It's one way of winning, of course. But I should not call it very sporting.'

He had struck the right note. The blush of shame mantled Sidney McMurdo's cheek. His hands fell to his sides, and he stood chewing his lip, plainly disconcerted.

'I hadn't looked at it like that,' he confessed.

'Posterity will,' said Harold Pickering.

'Yes, I see what you mean. Postpone it, then, you think, eh?'

'Indefinitely.'

'Oh, not indefinitely. We'll get together after the match. After all,' said Sidney McMurdo, looking on the bright side, 'it isn't long to wait.'

It was at this point that I joined them. As generally happened in those days, I had been given the honour of refereeing the final. I asked if they were ready to start.

'Not only ready,' said Sidney McMurdo. 'Impatient.'

Harold Pickering said nothing. He merely moistened the lips with the tip of the tongue.

My friends (proceeded the Oldest Member) have sometimes been kind enough to say that if there is one thing at which I excel, it is at describing in meticulous detail a desperately closely fought golf match – taking my audience stroke by stroke from tee one to hole eighteen and showing fortune fluctuating now to one side, now to the other, before finally placing the laurel wreath on the perspiring brow of the ultimate winner. And it is this treat that I should like to be able to give you now.

Unfortunately, the contest for that particular club championship final does not lend itself to such a description. From the very outset it was hopelessly one-sided.

Even as we walked to the first tee, it seemed to me that Harold Pickering was not looking his best and brightest. But I put this down to a nervous man's natural anxiety before an important match, and even when he lost the first two holes by the weakest type of play, I assumed that he would soon pull himself together and give of his best.

At that time, of course, I was not aware of the emotions surging in his bosom. It was only some years later that I ran into him and he told me his story and its sequel. That afternoon, what struck me most was the charming spirit of courtesy in which he played the match. He was losing every hole with monotonous regularity, and in such circumstances even the most amiable are apt to be gloomy and sullen, but he never lost his affability. He seemed to be straining every nerve to ingratiate himself with Sidney McMurdo and win the latter's affection.

Oddly, as it appeared to me then, it was McMurdo who was

sullen and gloomy. On three occasions he declined the offer of
a cigarette from his opponent, and was short in his manner – one
might almost say surly – when Harold Pickering, nine down at
the ninth, said that it was well worth anyone's while being beaten
by Sidney McMurdo because, apart from the fresh air and
exercise, it was such an artistic treat to watch his putting.

It was as he paid this graceful tribute that the crowd, which
had been melting away pretty steadily for the last quarter of an
hour, finally disappeared. By the time Sidney McMurdo had
holed out at the tenth for a four that gave him the match, we
were alone except for the caddies. These having been paid off,
we started to walk back.

To lose a championship match by ten and eight is an experience calculated to induce in a man an introspective silence, and
I had not expected Harold Pickering to contribute much to any
feast of reason and flow of soul which might enliven the homeward journey. To my surprise, however, as we started to cross
the bridge which spans the water at the eleventh, he burst into
animated speech, complimenting his conqueror in a graceful way
which I thought very sporting.

'I wonder if you will allow me to say, Mr McMurdo,' he began,
'how greatly impressed I have been by your performance this
afternoon. It has been a genuine revelation to me. It is so seldom
that one meets a man who, while long off the tee, also plays an
impeccable short game. I don't want to appear fulsome, but it
seems to me that you have everything.'

Words like these should have been music to Sidney Mc-
Murdo's ears, but he merely scowled darkly and uttered a short
grunt like a bulldog choking on a piece of steak.

'In fact, I don't mind telling you, McMurdo,' proceeded
Harold Pickering, still in that genial and ingratiating manner,

'that I shall watch your future career with considerable interest. It is a sad pity that this year's Walker Cup matches are over, for our team might have been greatly strengthened. Well, I venture to assert that next season the selection of at least one member will give the authorities little trouble.'

Sidney McMurdo uttered another grunt, and I saw what seemed like a look of discouragement come into Harold Pickering's face. But after gulping a couple of times he continued brightly.

'Tell me, Sidney,' he said, 'have you ever thought of writing a golf book? You know the sort of thing, old man. Something light and chatty, describing your methods and giving advice to the novice. If so, I should be delighted to publish it, and we should not quarrel about the terms. If I were you, I'd go straight home and start on it now.'

Sidney McMurdo spoke for the first time. His voice was deep and rumbling.

'I have something to do before I go home.'

'Oh, yes?'

'I am going to pound the stuffing out of a snake.'

'Ah, then in that case you will doubtless want to be alone, to concentrate. I will leave you.'

'No, you won't. Let us step behind those bushes for a moment, Mr Pickering,' said Sidney McMurdo.

I have always been good at putting two and two together, and listening to these exchanges I now sensed how matters stood. In a word, I saw all, and my heart bled for Harold Pickering. Unnecessarily, as it turned out, for even as my heart started to bleed, Harold Pickering acted.

I have said that we were crossing the bridge over the water at the eleventh, and no doubt you have been picturing that bridge as it is today – a stout steel structure. At the time of which I am speaking it was a mere plank with a rickety wooden rail along it, a rail ill adapted to withstand the impact of a heavy body.

Sidney McMurdo's was about as heavy a body as there was in the neighbourhood, and when Harold Pickering, with a resource and ingenuity which it would be difficult to overpraise, suddenly butted him in the stomach with his head and sent him reeling against it, it gave way without a moment's hesitation. There was a splintering crash, followed by a splash and a scurry of feet, and the next thing I saw was Harold Pickering disappearing over the horizon while Sidney McMurdo, up to his waist in water, petulantly detached an eel from his hair. It was a striking proof of the old saying that a publisher is never so dangerous as when apparently beaten. You may drive a publisher into a corner, but you do so at your own peril.

Presently, Sidney McMurdo waded ashore and started to slosh sullenly up the hillside towards the clubhouse. From the irritable manner in which he was striking himself between the shoulder blades I received the impression that he had got some sort of a water beetle down his back.

As I think I mentioned earlier, I did not see Harold Pickering again for some years, and it was only then that I was enabled to fill in the gaps in what has always seemed to me a singularly poignant human drama.

At first, he told me, he was actuated by the desire, which one can understand and sympathize with, to put as great a distance as possible between Sidney McMurdo and himself in the short-est possible time. With this end in view, he hastened to his car, which he had left standing outside the clubhouse, and placing a firm foot on the accelerator drove about seventy miles in the general direction of Scotland. Only when he paused for a sand-wich at a wayside tavern after completing this preliminary burst did he discover that all the money he had on his person was five shillings and a little bronze.

Now, a less agitated man would, of course, have seen that the policy to pursue was to take a room at a hotel, explain to the management that his luggage would be following shortly, and write to his bank to telegraph him such funds as he might require. But this obvious solution did not even occur to Harold Pickering. The only way out of the difficulty that suggested itself to him was to drive back to his cottage, secure the few pounds which he knew to be on the premises, throw into a suitcase some articles of clothing and his cheque book and then drive off again into the sunset.

As it happened, however, he would not have been able to drive into the sunset, for it was quite dark when he arrived at his destination. He alighted from his car, and was about to enter the house, when he suddenly observed that there was a light in the sitting-room. And creeping to the window and peering cautiously through a chink in the curtains, he saw that it was precisely as he had feared. There on a settee, scowling up at the ceiling, was Sidney McMurdo. He had the air of a man who was waiting for somebody.

And scarcely had Harold Pickering, appalled by this spectacle, withdrawn into a near-by bush to think the situation over in all of its aspects and try to find a formula, when heavy footsteps sounded on the gravel path and, dark though it was, he had no difficulty in identifying the newcomer as Agnes Flack. Only she could have clumped like that.

The next moment, she had delivered a resounding buffet on the front door, and Sidney McMurdo was opening it to her.

45

There was a silence as they gazed at one another. Except for that brief instant when she had introduced Harold Pickering to Sidney McMurdo outside the clubhouse, these sundered hearts had not met since the severance of their relations, and even a fifteen-stone man and an eleven-stone girl are not immune from embarrassment.

Agnes was the first to speak.

'Hullo,' she said. 'You here?'

'Yes,' said Sidney McMurdo, 'I'm here all right. I am waiting for the snake Pickering.'

'I've come to see him myself.'

'Oh? Well, nothing that you can do will save him from my wrath.'

'Who wants to save him from your wrath?'

'Don't you?'

'Certainly not. All I looked in for was to break our engagement.'

Sidney McMurdo staggered.

'Break your engagement?'

'That's right.'

'But I thought you loved him.'

'No more. The scales have fallen from my eyes. I don't marry men who are as hot as pistols in a friendly round with nothing depending on it, but blow up like geysers in competition golf. Why are you wrathful with him, Sidney?'

Sidney McMurdo gnashed his teeth.

'He stole you from me,' he said hoarsely.

If Agnes Flack had been about a foot shorter and had weighed about thirty pounds less, the sound which proceeded from her might have been described as a giggle. She stretched out the toe of her substantial shoe and made a squiggle with it on the gravel.

'And did you mind that so much?' she said softly, – or as softly as it was in her power to speak.

'Yes, I jolly well did,' said Sidney McMurdo. 'I love you, old girl, and I shall continue to love you till the cows come home. When I was demolishing the reptile Pickering this afternoon, your face seemed to float before me all the way round, even when I was putting. And I'll tell you something. I've been thinking it over, and I see now that I was all wrong that time and should unquestionably have used a Number Four iron. Too late, of course,' said Sidney McMurdo moodily, thinking of what might have been.

Agnes Flack drew a second arabesque on the gravel, using the toe of the other shoe this time.

'How do you mean, too late?' she asked reasonably softly.

'Well, isn't it too late?'

'Certainly not.'

'You can't mean you love me still?'

'Yes, I jolly well can mean I love you still.'

'Well, I'll be blowed! And here was I, thinking that all was over and life empty and all that sort of thing. My mate!' cried Sidney McMurdo.

They fell into an embrace like a couple of mastodons clashing in a primaeval swamp, and the earth had scarcely ceased to shake when a voice spoke.

'Excuse me.'

In his hiding-place in the bush Harold Pickering leaped as if somebody had touched off a land mine under his feet and came to rest quivering in every limb. He had recognized that voice.

'Excuse me,' said Troon Rockett. 'Does Mr Pickering live here?'

'Yes,' said Sidney McMurdo.

'If,' added Agnes Flack, 'you can call it living when a man enters for an important competition and gets beaten ten and eight. He's out at the moment. Better go in and stick around.'

'Thank you,' said the girl. 'I will.'

She vanished into the cottage. Sidney McMurdo took advantage of her departure to embrace Agnes Flack again.

'Old blighter,' he said tenderly, 'let's get married right away, before there can be any more misunderstandings and rifts and what not. How about Tuesday?'

'Can't Tuesday. Mixed foursomes.'

'Wednesday?'

'Can't Wednesday. Bogey competition.'

'And Thursday I'm playing in the invitation tournament at Squashy Heath,' said Sidney McMurdo. 'Oh, well, I daresay we shall manage to find a day when we're both free. Let's stroll along and talk it over.'

They crashed off, and as the echoes of their clumping feet died away in the distance Harold Pickering left the form in which he had been crouching and walked dizzily to the cottage. And the first thing he saw as he entered the sitting-room was Troon Rockett kissing a cabinet photograph of himself which she had taken from its place on the mantelpiece. The spectacle drew from him a sharp, staccato bark of amazement, and she turned, her eyes wide.

'Harold!' she cried, and flung herself into his arms.

To say that Harold Pickering was surprised, bewildered, startled and astounded would be merely to state the facts. He could not remember having been so genuinely taken aback since the evening when, sauntering in his garden in the dusk, he had trodden on the teeth of a rake and had the handle jump up and hit him on the nose.

But, as I have had occasion to observe before, he was a publisher, and I doubt if there is a publisher on the list who would not know what to do if a charming girl flung herself into his arms. I have told this story to one or two publishers of my acquaintance, and they all assured me that the correct procedure would come instinctively to them. Harold Pickering kissed Troon Rockett sixteen times in quick succession, and Macmillan and Faber and Faber say they would have done just the same.

At length, he paused. He was, as I have said, a man who liked to go into things.

'But I don't understand.'

'What don't you understand?'

'Well, don't think for a moment that I'm complaining, but this flinging-into-arms sequence strikes me as odd.'

'I can't imagine why. I love you.'

'But when I asked you to be my wife, you rose and walked haughtily from the room.'

'I didn't.'

'You did. I was there.'

'I mean, I didn't walk haughtily. I hurried out because I was alarmed and agitated. You sat there gasping and gurgling, and I thought you were having a fit of some kind. So I rushed off to phone the doctor, and when I got back you had gone. And then a day or two later another man proposed to me, and he, too, started gasping and gurgling, and I realized the truth. They told me at your office that you were living here, so I came along to let you know that I loved you.'

'You really do?'

'Of course I do. I loved you the first moment I saw you. You remember? You were explaining to father that thirteen copies count as twelve, and I came in and our eyes met. In that instant I knew that you were the only man in the world for me.'

For a moment Harold Pickering was conscious only of a wild exhilaration. He felt as if his firm had brought out *Gone With the Wind*. Then a dull, hopeless look came into his sensitive face.

'It can never be,' he said.

'Why not?'

'You heard what that large girl was saying outside there, but probably you did not take it in. It was the truth. I was beaten this afternoon ten and eight.'

'Everybody has an off day.'

He shook his head.

'It was not an off day. That was my true form. I haven't the nerve to be a scratch man. When the acid test comes, I blow up. I suppose I'm about ten, really. You can't marry a ten-handicap man.'

'Why not?'

'You! The daughter of John Rockett and his British Ladies Champion wife. The great-granddaughter of old Ma Rockett. The sister of Prestwick, Sandwich, Hoylake and St Andrew Rockett.'

'But that's just why. It has always been my dream to marry a man with a handicap of about ten, so that we could go through life together side by side, twin souls. I should be ten, if the family didn't make me practise five hours a day all the year round. I'm not a natural scratch. I have made myself scratch by ceaseless, unremitting toil, and if there's one thing in the world I loathe it is ceaseless, unremitting toil. The relief of being able to let myself slip back to ten is indescribable. Oh, Harold, we shall be so happy. Just to think of taking three putts on a green! It will be heaven!'

Harold Pickering had been reeling a good deal during these remarks. He now ceased to do so. There is a time for reeling and a time for not reeling.

'You mean that?'

'I certainly do.'

'You will really marry me?'

'How long does it take to get a licence?'

For an instant Harold Pickering sought for words, but found none. Then a rather neat thing that Sidney McMurdo had said came back to him. Sidney McMurdo was a man he could never really like, but his dialogue was excellent.

'My mate!' he said.

3 THE RIGHT APPROACH

The subject of magazine stories came up quite suddenly in the bar parlour of the Angler's Rest, as subjects are wont to do there, for in the way the minds of our little group flit from this topic to that there is always a suggestion of the chamois of the Alps springing from crag to crag. We were, if I remember rightly, discussing supralapsarianism, when a Whisky-and-Splash, who had been turning the pages of the *Saturday Evening Post*, the property of our courteous and popular barmaid Miss Postlethwaite, uttered a snort.

'Gesundheit,' said a Draught Ale.

'I wasn't sneezing, I was snorting,' said the Whisky-and-Splash. Disgustedly, he added, 'Why do they publish these things?'

'What things would that be?'

'These stories, illustrated in glorious Technicolor, where the fellow meets the girl on the beach, and they start kidding back and forth, and twenty minutes after they've seen each other for the first time, they're engaged to be married.'

Mr Mulliner took a sip from his hot Scotch and lemon.

'You find that unconvincing?'

'Yes, I do. I am a married man, and it took me two years and more boxes of chocolates than I care to think of to persuade the lady who is now my wife to sign on the dotted line. And though it is not for me to say so, I was a pretty fascinating chap in those days. Ask anybody.'

Mr Mulliner nodded.

'Your point is well taken. But you must make allowances for the editor of the *Saturday Evening Post*. He lives in a world of his own, and really does think that two complete strangers can meet in bathing suits on the beach and conclude their initial conversation by becoming betrothed. However, as you say, it seldom happens in ordinary life. Even the Mulliners, most of whom have fallen in love at first sight, have not found the going quite so smooth and simple as that. They have been compelled to pull up their socks and put in not a little preliminary spade-work. The case of my nephew Augustus is one that springs to the mind.'

'Did he meet girls in bathing suits on beaches?'

'Frequently. But it was at a charity bazaar at a house called Balmoral on Wimbledon Common that love came to him, for it was there that he saw Hermione Brimble and fell with a thud that could have been heard as far off as Putney Hill.'

It was owing to his godmother's fondness for bazaars (said Mr Mulliner) that Augustus found himself in the garden of Balmoral, and it is ironical to reflect that when she ordered him to escort her there, he was considerably annoyed, for he had been planning to go to Kempton Park and with word and gesture encourage in the two-thirty race a horse in whose fortunes he was interested. But his chagrin was not long-lasting. What caused it to vanish was the sight of a girl so divine that, as his gaze rested upon her, the top hat rocked on his head and only a sudden snatch at the last moment prevented his umbrella from falling from his grip.

'Well, well,' he said to himself, as he drank her in, 'this certainly opens up a new line of thought.'

She was presiding over a stall in the shade of a large cedar at the edge of the lawn, and as soon as he could get his limbs to function he hastened up and began buying everything in sight. And when a tea-cosy, two Teddy bears, a penwiper, a bowl of wax flowers and a fretwork pipe-rack had changed hands he felt that he was entitled to regard himself as a member of the club and get friendly.

'Lovely day,' he said.

'Beautiful,' said the girl.

'The sun,' said Augustus, pointing it out with his umbrella.

The girl said Yes, she had noticed the sun.

'I always think it seems to make everything so much brighter, if you know what I mean, when the sun's shining,' said Augustus. 'Well, it's been awfully jolly, meeting you. My name, in case you're interested, is Mulliner.'

The girl said hers was Hermione Brimble, and further enquiry elicited the fact that she lived there with her Aunt, Mrs Willoughby Gudgeon. And Augustus was wondering if he could start calling her Hermione right away, or whether it would be better to wait for a few minutes, when a formidable woman of the heavy-battlecruiser class came rolling up.

'Well, dear,' she said. 'How are you doing?'

The girl, addressing the newcomer as Aunt Beatrice, replied that the market had opened easy, but that sales had recently been stepped up by the arrival of a big-time operator. 'Mr Mulliner,' she said, indicating Augustus, who was standing on one leg, looking ingratiating.

'Mulliner?' said Mrs Gudgeon. 'Are you related to the Bishop of Bognor? He was the Rev. Theophilus Mulliner. We were great friends when I was a girl.'

It was the first time that Augustus had heard of this prelate, but he was not going to pass up the smallest chance of furthering his interests.

'Oh, rather. A cousin. But I always call him Uncle Phil.'

'I have not seen him for some time. How is he these days?'

'Oh, fine. Full of yeast.'

'I am relieved to hear it. He used to be troubled a good deal by clergyman's sore throat, like my niece Hermione's father, the late Bishop of Stortford,' said Mrs Gudgeon, and it was at this moment that Augustus came to the decision which was to plunge him into what Shakespeare calls a sea of troubles.

This girl, he told himself, was the daughter of a bishop and looked like something out of a stained-glass window, a pure white soul if he ever saw one. Her aunt was the sort of woman who went around with gangs of the higher clergy. Obviously, then, what would establish him as a desirable suitor was saintly rectitude. His until now had been a somewhat rackety life, including no fewer than three fines for disorderly conduct on Boat Race Night, but he resolved from even date to be so saintly and so rectitudinous that both the girl and her aunt would draw in their breath with an awed 'What ho!' as he did his stuff.

Taking as his cue a statement on the part of the latter that this bazaar was in aid of the Wimbledon Social Purity League, he hitched up his diaphragm and let himself go. He said he was glad they were giving Social Purity a break because he was strong for it and always had been. There was a type of young man, he went on, who would not recognize Social Purity if you handed it to him on a skewer, and it was a type he had always avoided.

Give him fine weather and a spot of Social Purity, he said, and you need not worry about him any further. You could just leave him, he said, confident that he was having the time of his life. And it was not long before he was receiving from Mrs Willoughby Gudgeon a cordial invitation to haunt the house, an invitation of which he was determined to avail himself freely.

Into the events of the next few weeks it is not necessary for me to go in detail. Suffice it to say that at his every visit to Balmoral Augustus displayed an all-in saintliness which would have caused comment at a Pan-Anglican Synod. He brought the girl serious books. He spoke of his ideals. On several occasions at luncheon he declined a second go at the roast duck and peas or whatever it might be, indicating by his manner that all that sort of thing seemed to him a little gross and unspiritual. And it was clear to him that in supposing that this was the stuff to give them he had not been mistaken. He would sometimes catch the girl looking at him in a strange, thoughtful way, as if she were asking herself if he could really be true, and he was convinced that love was burgeoning.

At the outset of his wooing he had had some anxious moments owing to the constant presence at Balmoral of Mrs Gudgeon's stepson, Oswald Stoker, a young man who wrote novels and, differing in this respect from the great majority of novelists, looked not like something brought in by a not too fastidious cat but was extremely personable. He was also gay and debonair. He did not live at Balmoral, but he was frequently there, and every time his visits coincided with those of Augustus the latter was pained to observe the cordiality of his relations with Hermione.

Of course, they were sort of cousins, and you have to allow sort of cousins a bit of leeway, but still he did not like it, and it was with profound relief that he learned one day that Oswald was earmarked elsewhere, being betrothed to a girl named Yvonne something who was connected with the television industry. It changed his whole view of the man. He could see now that Oswald Stoker was a charming chap, with whom he might easily form a beautiful friendship, and when one afternoon arriving at Balmoral for the day's haunting, he found him in the drawing-room with Hermione, he greeted him warmly and enquired solicitously after his health.

'My health,' said Oswald Stoker, having thanked him for asking, 'is at present excellent, but who can predict how I shall be feeling this time tomorrow? I have stern work before me this night, Mulliner. Russell Clutterbuck, my American publisher, is in London, and I am dining with him. Have you ever dined with Russell Clutterbuck?'

Augustus said that he had not the pleasure of Mr Clutterbuck's acquaintance.

'It's an experience,' said Oswald Stoker moodily, and left the room shaking his head.

His new affection for the novelist made Augustus feel concerned. He said he was afraid Oswald was worried, and Hermione sighed.

'He is thinking of the last time he dined with Mr Clutterbuck.'

'What happened?'

'He is vague on the subject. He says his memory is blurred. All he can recall is waking next morning on the floor of his bed-room and shooting up to the ceiling when a sparrow on the window-sill chirped unexpectedly. Gave his head a nasty bump, he tells me.'

'You mean that on the previous night he had over-indulged?'

'The evidence would seem to point that way.'

'Tck, tck!'

'It shocks you?'

'It does a little, I confess. I have never been able to understand what pleasure men can find in spirituous liquors. Lemonade is so much more refreshing. I drink nothing else myself.'

'But you're different.'

'I suppose so.'

'You are so good and steady,' said Hermione, giving him that strange, thoughtful look of hers.

It seemed to Augustus that he could scarcely want a better cue than this. He tried, but failed, to take her little hand in his.

'Hermione,' he said, 'I love you.'

'Oh, yes?' said Hermione.

'Will you marry me?'

'No,' said Hermione.

Augustus stared, amazed.

'No?'

'No.'

'You mean you won't marry me?'

Hermione said that that put in a nutshell exactly what she was trying to convey. She then gazed at him, gave a little shudder, and left the room.

All through the day and far into the night Augustus sat in his rooms brooding on the girl's extraordinary attitude, and the more he brooded on it, the more baffling did it appear. She had bewildered him. He reviewed his behaviour of the last few weeks, and if ever there was behaviour calculated to make the daughter of a bishop feel that here was her destined mate, this behaviour, he considered, was that behaviour. If she was not satisfied with the Augustus Mulliner of his Wimbledon period, all one could say was that she must be holding out for something pretty super.

It was towards one in the morning that he came to the conclusion that she had not meant what she said, maidenly modesty having caused her to fluff her lines, and he decided that this theory must be tested immediately. The hour was a little advanced, but your impetuous lover does not keep his eye on the clock. Augustus, like all the Mulliners, was a man of action. He sprang from his chair, sprang for his hat, sprang into the street, sprang into a passing taxi, and some forty minutes later was ringing the front door bell of Balmoral.

After a considerable interval the door was opened by Staniforth, the butler, in pyjamas and a dressing-gown. His manner seemed a little short, Augustus was unable to think why, and it was almost curtly that he informed my nephew that Mrs Gudgeon and Hermione were attending the Social Purity Ball at the Town Hall and would not be back for some time.

'I'll come in and wait,' said Augustus.

He was in error. Even as he spoke, the door slammed, leaving him alone in the silent night.

An ardent swain who is left alone in the silent night in the garden of the aunt of the girl he loves does not say to himself 'Ho, hum. Well, better call it a day, I suppose' and go home to bed. He backs away from the house and stands gazing reverently up at her window. And if, like Augustus, he does not know which her window is, he gazes reverently at all the windows, taking them in rotation. Augustus was doing this, and had just shifted his eye from the top left second window to the top left third window, when a voice spoke behind him, causing him to break the European record for the standing high jump.

'Ah, Mulliner, old friend,' said Oswald Stoker, for the voice was his, 'I thought I should find you here. Gazing at her window, eh? Very natural. In my courting days I used to do a lot of window-gazing. There is no healthier pursuit. Keeps you out in the open and fills your lungs with fresh air. Harley Street physicians recommend it. But is window-gazing enough? That is what we must ask ourselves. I say no. You need a better approach. In this matter of wooing, everything, I contend, turns on getting the right approach, and this, my dear Mulliner, you have not yet got. I have watched with a fatherly eye your passion for my step-cousin or whatever the hell she is, and it has amazed me that you have overlooked the one essential factor in winning a girl's heart. I allude to the serenade. Have you ever stood beneath her window and to the accompaniment of a banjo begged her to throw you down one little rose from her hair? To the best of my knowledge, no. You should iron out this bug in the production at the earliest possible moment, Mulliner, if you want the thing to be a success.'

Augustus did not at all like having his great love subjected to analysis by one who, after all, was a comparative stranger, but his mind at the moment was occupied with another aspect of the matter. The visibility was too poor for him to see his companion's face, but there was that in the timbre of his voice which enabled him to form a swift diagnosis. He had had countless opportunities of studying the symptoms, and it was plain to him that the man, if not yet actually ossified, was indubitably plastered. Yielding to the dictates of his lower nature, he must for some hours have been mopping up the stuff like a suction pump.

Oswald Stoker seemed to sense the silent criticism, for it was on this that he now touched.

'It has probably not escaped you, Mulliner, that I am a trifle under the influence of the sauce. As who would not be after spending the evening with Russell Clutterbuck, of the firm of

Winch and Clutterbuck, Madison Avenue, New York, publishers of the book beautiful. I suppose there is no wilder Indian
than an American publisher, when he gets off the reservation.
Relieved for the nonce of the nauseous daily task of interviewing
American authors, most of them wearing horn-rimmed spectacles, he has an exhilarating sense of freedom. He expands. He
lets himself go. Well, when I tell you that in a few short hours
Russell Clutterbuck got self and guest thrown out of three
grillrooms and a milk bar, you will appreciate what I mean.
Rightly or wrongly, he feels that electric fans are placed there to
have eggs thrown at them, and he saw to it that before we started
making the rounds he was well supplied with these. He kept
showing me how a baseball pitcher winds up and propels the
ball. Speed and control, he told me, are what you have to have.'

'You must be glad to have seen the last of him.'

'I haven't seen the last of him. I brought him here to show him
the spot where I played as a child. I didn't really play here as a
child, because we lived at Cheltenham, but he won't know the
difference. He's out there somewhere, exercising the dog.'

'The dog?'

'He bought a dog earlier in the evening. He generally makes
some such purchase on these occasions. I have known him to
buy an ostrich. I suppose I had better be going and looking for
him,' said Oswald Stoker, and vanished into the darkness.

It was perhaps two minutes later that the dog to which he had
alluded suddenly entered Augustus's life.

It was a large, uncouth dog, in its physique and deportment
not unlike the hound of the Baskervilles, though of course not
covered with phosphorus, and it seemed to be cross about something. Its air was that of a dog which has discovered plots against
its person, and it appeared to be under the impression that in

Augustus it had found one of the ringleaders, for the menace in its manner, as it now advanced on him, was unmistakable. A few words of explanation might have convinced the animal of my nephew's innocence, but Augustus deemed it wisest not to linger and deliver them. To climb the nearest tree was the work of an instant. It happened, oddly enough, to be the very cedar in the shade of which in happier days Hermione Brimble had sold him a tea-cosy, two Teddy bears, a penwiper, a bowl of wax fruit and a fretwork pipe-rack.

He crouched there in the upper branches while the dog, seeming puzzled, as if unused to having members of the underworld take to themselves the wings of a dove, paced to and fro like a man looking for a dropped collar-stud. Presently it abandoned the search and trotted off with a muffled oath, and some little time after that Augustus, peering down from his eyrie, saw Oswald Stoker returning, accompanied by a very stout man holding a bottle of champagne by the neck and singing the Star-Spangled Banner. They halted beneath the tree.

It would have been possible for Augustus at this juncture to have made his presence known, but something told him that the less he had to do with Oswald Stoker in his present unbalanced condition, the better. He continued crouching, therefore, in silence, and Oswald Stoker spoke.

'Well, well,' he said, 'my young friend Mulliner, of whom I was speaking to you just now, appears to have left us. I was telling you, if you remember, of his great love for my step-cousin Hermione and of my wish to do all that lies in my power to promote his interests. Your singing reminds me that the first step, the serenade, has yet to be taken. No doubt you are about to draw to my attention the fact that he can't serenade her, if he isn't here. Very true. But what happens in the theatre when the star

is absent? You put on an understudy. I propose to step into the
breach and take his place. It would be more effective, of course,
had I some musical instrument such as a clavichord or sackbut
on which to accompany myself, but if you would hum the bass,
I think the performance should be adequate. I beg your pardon?'

Mr Clutterbuck had muttered something about launching the
ship. He shook his head, as if demurring.

'Gotta launch ship first,' he said. 'Customary ceremony,' and
raising the bottle he held he flung it adroitly through the pane
of one of the upper windows.

'Good luck to all who sail in you,' he said.

It was Oswald Stoker's turn to shake his head.

'Now there, my dear fellow, if you don't mind me saying so,
I think you deviated from the usual programme. It is surely the
bottle, not the ship that should be broken. However,' he went
on, as the upper slopes of Staniforth the butler thrust themselves
out of the window, 'it has produced results. We have assembled
an audience. You were saying?' he said, addressing Staniforth.

The butler, like the dog, seemed to be cross about something.

'Who,' he demanded, 'is there?'

'Augustus Mulliner speaking. Or, rather,' said Oswald Stoker,
starting to do so, 'singing.'

The sight of the protruding head had had the effect of stirring
Mr Clutterbuck to give of his best. Once more Oswald Stoker
was privileged to witness his impersonation of a baseball pitcher
winding up, which in its essentials rather closely resembles the
first stages of an epileptic fit. The next moment an egg, unerr-
ingly aimed, had found its target.

'Right in the groove,' said Mr Clutterbuck contentedly. He
wandered off, conscious of a good night's work done, and
Oswald Stoker had scarcely had time to light a cigarette and

A FEW QUICK ONES

enjoy a few refreshing puffs when he was joined by Mrs Gudgeon's major-domo, carrying a shot gun.

'Ah, Staniforth,' he said genially. 'Out for a day with the birds?'

'Good evening, Mr Stoker. I am looking for Mr Mulliner,' said the butler with cold menace.

'Mulliner, eh? He was here a moment ago. I remember noticing. You want him for some special reason?'

'I think he should be overpowered and placed under restraint before the ladies return.'

'Why, what has he been doing?'

'He sang beneath my window.'

'Rather a compliment. What was the burden of his song?'

'As far as I could understand him, he was requesting me to throw him a rose from my hair.'

'You didn't?'

'No, sir.'

'Quite right. Roses cost money.'

'He also threw an egg at me.'

'So that is why you have so much yolk on your face. I thought it might be one of those beauty treatments, like the mud-pack. Ah well, young blood, Staniforth.'

'Sir?'

'At Mulliner's age one has these ebullitions of high spirits. Much must be excused in the young.'

'Not singing under windows and throwing eggs at three in the morning.'

'No, there perhaps he went too far. He has been a little over-excited all the evening. We dined together, and he got us bounced in rapid succession from three grillrooms and a milk bar. Would keep throwing eggs at the electric fan. Hullo!' said

Oswald Stoker, as a distant splash sounded in the night. 'I think a friend of mine has fallen in the pond. I will go and investigate. He may need a helping hand.'

He hurried off, and Augustus was glad to see him go. But his pleasure was rendered imperfect by the fact that the butler did not follow his example. Staniforth had plainly decided to make a night of it. He remained *in statu quo*, and presently there was the sound of a vehicle stopping at the gate, and Mrs Gudgeon and Hermione came walking down the drive.

'Staniforth!' the former cried. It was a novel experience for her to find the domestic staff prowling the grounds in the small hours, and Augustus received the impression that if she had been less carefully brought up and had known fewer bishops, she would have said 'Gorblimey!'.

'Good evening, madam.'

'What are you doing out here at this time?'

'I am pursuing Mr Mulliner, madam.'

'Pursuing *what*?'

The butler, having paused for a moment, as if asking himself if 'whom' would not have been more correct, repeated his statement.

'But Mr Mulliner is not here?'

'Yes, madam.'

'At three o'clock in the morning?'

'Yes, madam. He called shortly before two, and rang the front-door bell. I informed him that you were not at home, and supposed that he had left the premises. Such, however, was not the case. Ten minutes ago he flung a bottle of champagne through my window, and when I looked out expressed a wish that I would throw him a rose from my hair. He then hit me in the left eye with an egg.'

It seemed to Augustus that he heard Hermione utter a startled cry, but it was lost in Mrs Gudgeon's snort of amazement.

'Mr *Mulliner* did this?'

'Yes, madam. I gather from Mr Stoker, with whom I was conversing a short while ago, that his behaviour throughout the evening has been on similar lines. He was a member of the dinner party which Mr Stoker attended, and Mr Stoker tells me that he was instrumental in getting himself and friends ejected from three grillrooms and a milk bar. Mr Stoker attributed his exuberance to youthful high spirits, and advanced the suggestion that such conduct should be excused in the young. I must confess that I am unable to take so liberal a view.'

Mrs Gudgeon was silent for some moments. She appeared to be trying to adjust her mind to these revelations. It is never easy for a woman to realize that she has been nursing in her bosom, which is practically what she had been doing to my nephew Augustus, a viper. But presently the adjusting process seemed to be complete. She spoke grimly.

'Next time Mr Mulliner calls, Staniforth, I am not at home. . . . What was that?'

'Madam?'

'I thought I heard a moan.'

'The breeze sighing in the trees, no doubt, madam.'

'Perhaps you are right. The breeze does sigh in trees, frequently. Did you hear it, Hermione?'

'I thought I heard something.'

'A moan?'

'A groan, I should have said.'

'A moan or groan,' said Mrs Gudgeon, conceding the point. 'As if wrenched from the lips of some soul in agony.' She broke off as a figure came out of the shadows. 'Oswald!'

Oswald Stoker waved a genial hand.

'Hullo there. Hullo, hullo, hullo, hullo.'

'What are you doing here?'

'Just winding up the evening. Oh, before I forget, my publisher fell into the pond and is now in the hothouse, drying out. So if you go there and see a nude publisher, pretend not to notice.'

'Oswald, you are intoxicated!'

'It is virtually impossible not to be,' said Oswald Stoker gravely, 'when you have been entertained at dinner by Russell Clutterbuck of Clutterbuck and Winch, publishers of the book beautiful, and your fellow guest is Augustus Mulliner. I'm looking for him, by the way. I want to warn him that there is a herd of purple rhinoceroses down by the pond. Very dangerous things, purple rhinoceroses, especially in the mating season. Bite you in the leg as soon as look at you.'

Hermione spoke. Her voice shook.

'Oswald!'

'Hullo?'

'Is this true what Staniforth has been saying about Mr Mulliner?'

'What did he say?'

'That Mr Mulliner sang under his window and threw eggs at him?'

'Perfectly correct. I was an eyewitness.'

Mrs Gudgeon swelled formidably.

'I shall write Mr Mulliner a very strong letter tomorrow. In the third person. He shall never enter this house again ... There! I'm sure that was a moan. I wonder if the garden is haunted.'

She turned away, and Oswald Stoker regarded her anxiously.

'You aren't going to the hothouse?'

'I am going to my room. Bring me a glass of warm milk there, Staniforth.'

'Very good, madam.'

She moved off toward the house, followed by the butler, and Oswald Stoker, turning to Hermione, was concerned to find her shaking with uncontrollable sobs.

'Hullo!' he said. 'Something wrong?'

The girl gulped like a leaky radiator.

'You bet your Old Etonian sock suspenders there's something wrong. I have lost the man I love.'

'Where did you see him last?'

'How was I to know,' Hermione went on, her voice vibrating with pain, 'that – that was the sort of ball of fire Augustus Mulliner really was? I thought him a wet smack and a total loss, and all the time he was a sportsman who throws eggs at butlers and breaks windows with champagne bottles. I never dreamed that there was this deeper side to him. When first we met, I was strangely attracted to him, but as I came to know him, he appeared to have all the earmarks of a Grade A hammerhead. I wrote him off as a bohunkus. Romantically considered, he seemed to me strictly a cigar-store Indian, all wood from the neck up. And now I see that for some reason he was hiding his light beneath a bushel, as father used to say. Oh, what shall I do? I love him, I love him, I love him!'

'Well, he loves you, which makes it all square.'

'Yes, but this afternoon he asked me to be his wife, and I turned him down like a bedspread.'

'Send him a civil note, saying you have changed your mind.'

'Too late. A man as fascinating as that is sure to have been snapped up by some other girl by this time. Oh, what . . . ?'

She would have spoken further, probably adding the words

'shall I do?', but at this moment speech was wiped from her lips as if with a wet sponge. From the tree in whose shade she stood a passionate voice had shouted 'Hoy!' and looking up she saw the face of my nephew.

'Au-us-us!' she cried. His sudden advent had caused her to bite her tongue rather severely.

'Ah, Mulliner,' said Oswald Stoker. 'Birds-nesting?'

'I say,' bellowed Augustus, 'I heard what you were saying. Did you mean it?'

'Yek, yek, a 'ousand 'imes yek!'

'You really love me?'

'Of course I love you.'

'You will be my wife?'

'You couldn't stop me with an injunction.'

'Then . . . just getting it straightened out, if you don't mind . . . it will be in order if I nip down and cover your upturned face with burning kisses?'

'Perfectly in order.'

'Right ho. Be with you in a moment.'

As they fell into an embrace which, had it occurred in a motion picture, would have made the Johnston office purse its lips and suggest the cutting of several hundred feet of film, Oswald Stoker heaved a sentimental little sigh. A fiancé himself, he liked to see sundered hearts coming together.

'Well, well!' he said. 'So you're getting married, eh? Starting out on the new life, are you, you two young things? Then take this simple toad,' said Oswald Stoker, pressing the reptile into Augustus's hand. 'A wedding present,' he explained. 'A poor gift, but one that comes straight from the heart. And, after all, it's the thought behind the gift that counts, don't you think? Good-night. God bless you. I must be getting along and finding how Russell Clutterbuck is making out. Have you ever seen an American publisher sitting in a hothouse with nothing on except horn-rimmed spectacles? It is a sight well worth seeing, but not one that I would recommend to nervous people and invalids.'

He passed into the darkness, leaving Augustus looking at the toad a little dubiously. He did not really want it, but it might be ungracious to throw it away.

An idea struck him.

'Darling!'

'Yes, Angel?'

'I wonder, my queen, if you know which is that butler's room?'

'Of course, my king. Why?'

'I thought if you were to put this toad in his bed some night, shortly before he retired to rest ... Just a suggestion, of course.'

'An admirable suggestion. Come, my dream man,' said Hermione, 'and let us hunt around and see if we can't find a few frogs, too.'

In these disturbed days in which we live, it has probably occurred to all thinking men that something drastic ought to be done about aunts. Speaking for myself, I have long felt that stones should be turned and avenues explored with a view to putting a stopper on the relatives in question. If someone were to come to me and say, 'Wooster, would you be interested in joining a society I am starting whose aim will be the suppression of aunts or at least will see to it that they are kept on a short chain and not permitted to roam hither and thither at will, scattering desolation on all sides?', I would reply, 'Wilbraham,' if his name was Wilbraham, 'I am with you heart and soul. Put me down as a foundation member.' And my mind would flit to the sinister episode of my Aunt Dahlia and the Fothergill Venus, from which I am making only a slow recovery. Whisper the words 'Marsham Manor' in my ear, and I still quiver like a humming-bird.

At the time of its inception, if inception is the word I want, I was, I recall, feeling at the top of my form and without a care in the world. Pleasantly relaxed after thirty-six holes of golf and dinner at the Drones, I was lying on the *chez Wooster* sofa doing the *Telegraph* crossword puzzle, when the telephone rang. I could hear Jeeves out in the hall dealing with it, and presently he trickled in.

'Mrs Travers, sir.'

'Aunt Dahlia? What does she want?'

'She did not confide in me, sir. But she appears anxious to establish communication with you.'

'To talk to me, do you mean?'

'Precisely, sir.'

A bit oddish it seems to me, looking back on it, that as I went to the instrument I should have had no premonition of an impending doom. Not psychic, that's my trouble. Having no inkling of the soup into which I was so shortly to be plunged, I welcomed the opportunity of exchanging ideas with this sister of my late father who, as is widely known, is my good and deserving aunt, not to be confused with Aunt Agatha, the werewolf. What with one thing and another, it was some little time since we had chewed the fat together.

'What ho, old blood relation,' I said.

'Hullo, Bertie, you revolting young blot,' she responded in her hearty way. 'Are you sober?'

'As a judge.'

'Then listen attentively. I'm speaking from an under-sized hamlet in Hampshire called Marsham-in-the-Vale. I'm staying at Marsham Manor with Cornelia Fothergill, the novelist. Ever heard of her?'

'Vaguely, as it were. She is not on my library list.'

'She would be, if you were a woman. She specializes in rich goo for the female trade.'

'Ah, yes, like Mrs Bingo Little. Rosie M. Banks to you.'

'That sort of thing, yes, but even goo-ier. Where Rosie M. Banks merely touches the heart strings, Cornelia Fothergill grabs them in both hands and ties them into knots. I'm trying to talk her into letting me have her new novel as a serial for the *Boudoir*.'

I got the gist. She has since sold it, but at the time of which I speak this aunt was the proprietor or proprietress of a weekly paper for the half-witted woman called *Milady's Boudoir*, to which I once contributed an article – a 'piece' we old hands call it – on What The Well-Dressed Man Is Wearing. Like all weekly papers, it was in the process of turning the corner, as the expression is, and I could well understand that a serial by a specialist in rich goo would give it a much-needed shot in the arm.

'How's it coming?' I asked. 'Any luck?'

'Not so far. She demurs.'

'Dewhat's?'

'Murs, you silly ass.'

'You mean she meets your pleas with what Jeeves would call a *nolle prosequi*?'

'Not quite that. She has not closed the door to a peaceful settlement, but, as I say, she de—'

'Murs?'

'Murs is right. She doesn't say No, but she won't say Yes. The trouble is that Tom is doing his Gaspard-the-Miser stuff again.'

Her allusion was to my uncle, Thomas Portarlington Travers, who foots the bills for what he always calls *Madame's Nightshirt*. He is as rich as creosote, as I believe the phrase is, but like so many of our wealthier citizens he hates to give up. Until you have heard Uncle Tom on the subject of income tax and supertax, you haven't heard anything.

'He won't let me go above five hundred pounds, and she wants eight.'

'Looks like an impasse.'

'It did till this morning.'

'What happened this morning?'

'Oh, just a sort of break in the clouds. She said something

which gave me the impression that she was weakening and that one more shove would do the trick. Are you still sober?'

'I am.'

'Then keep so over this next week-end, because you're coming down here.'

'Who, me?'

'You, in person.'

'But, why?'

'To help me sway her. You will exercise all your charm—'

'I haven't much.'

'Well, exercise what you've got. Give her the old oil. Play on her as on a stringed instrument.'

I chewed the lip somewhat. I'm not keen on these blind dates. And if life has taught me one thing, it is that the prudent man keeps away from female novelists. But it might be, of course, that a gay house-party was contemplated. I probed her on this point.

'Will anyone else be there? Is there any bright young society, I mean?'

'I wouldn't call the society young, but it's very bright. There's Cornelia's husband, Everard Fothergill the artist, and his father Edward Fothergill. He's an artist, too, of a sort. You won't have a dull moment. So tell Jeeves to pack your effects, and we shall expect you on Friday. You will continue to haunt the house till Monday.'

'Cooped up with a couple of artists and a writer of rich goo? I don't like it.'

'You don't have to like it,' the aged relative assured me. 'You just do it. Oh, and by the way, when you get here, I've a little something I want you to do for me.'

'What sort of a little something?'

'I'll tell you about it when I see you. Just a simple little thing

to help Auntie. You'll enjoy it,' she said, and with a cordial
'Toodle-oo' rang off.

It surprises many people, I believe, that Bertram Wooster, as a
general rule a man of iron, is as wax in the hands of his Aunt
Dahlia, jumping to obey her lightest behest like a performing
seal going after a slice of fish. They do not know that this woman
possesses a secret weapon by means of which she can always bend
me to her will – viz. the threat that if I give her any of my lip,
she will bar me from her dinner table and deprive me of the roasts
and boileds of her French chef Anatole, God's gift to the gastric
juices. When she says Go, accordingly, I do not demur, I goeth,
as the Bible puts it, and so it came about that toward the quiet
evenfall of Friday the 22nd inst. I was at the wheel of the old
sports model, tooling through Hants with Jeeves at my side and
weighed down with a nameless foreboding.

'Jeeves,' I said, 'I am weighed down with a nameless foreboding.'

'Indeed, sir?'

'Yes. What, I ask myself, is cooking?'

'I do not think I quite follow you, sir.'

'Then you jolly well ought to. I reported my conversation with
Aunt Dahlia to you verbatim, and you should have every word of
it tucked away beneath your bowler hat. To refresh your memory,
after a certain amount of kidding back and forth she said "I've a
little something I want you to do for me", and when I enquired
what, she fobbed me off ... is it fobbed?'

'Yes, sir.'

'She fobbed me off with a careless "Oh, just a simple little
thing to help Auntie". What construction do you place on those
words?'

'One gathers that there is something Mrs Travers wishes you to do for her, sir.'

'One does, but the point is – what? You recall what has happened in the past when the gentler sex have asked me to do things for them. Especially Aunt Dahlia. You have not forgotten the affair of Sir Watkyn Basset and the silver cow-creamer?'

'No, sir.'

'On that occasion, but for you, Bertram Wooster would have done a stretch in the local hoosegow. Who knows that this little something to which she referred will not land me in a similar peril? I wish I could slide out of this binge, Jeeves.'

'I can readily imagine it, sir.'

'But I can't, I'm like those Light Brigade fellows. You remember how matters stood with them?'

'Very vividly, sir. Theirs not to reason why, theirs but to do and die.'

'Exactly. Cannons to right of them, cannons to left of them volleyed and thundered, but they had to keep snapping into it regardless. I know just how they felt,' I said, moodily stepping on the accelerator. The brow was furrowed and the spirits low.

Arrival at Marsham Manor did little to smooth the former and raise the latter. Shown into the hall, I found myself in as cosy an interior as one could wish – large log fire, comfortable chairs and a tea-table that gave out an invigorating aroma of buttered toast and muffins, all very pleasant to encounter after a long drive on a chilly winter afternoon – but a single glance at the personnel was enough to tell me that I had struck one of those joints where every prospect pleases and only man is vile.

Three human souls were present when I made my entry, each

plainly as outstanding a piece of cheese as Hampshire could provide. One was a small, thin citizen with a beard of the type that causes so much distress – my host, I presumed – and seated near him was another bloke of much the same construction but an earlier model, whom I took to be the father. He, too, was bearded to the gills. The third was a large spreading woman wearing the horn-rimmed spectacles which are always an occupational risk for penpushers of the other sex. They gave her a rather remarkable resemblance to my Aunt Agatha, and I would be deceiving my public were I to say that the heart did not sink to some extent. To play on such a woman as on a stringed instrument wasn't going to be the simple task Aunt Dahlia appeared to think it.

After a brief pause for station identification, she introduced me to the gang, and I was on the point of doing the civil thing by asking Everard Fothergill if he had been painting anything lately, when he stiffened.

'Hark!' he said. 'Can you hear a mewing cat?'

'Eh?' I said.

'A mewing cat. I feel sure I hear a mewing cat. Listen!'

While we were listening the door opened and Aunt Dahlia came in. Everard put the 64,000-dollar question squarely up to her.

'Mrs Travers, did you meet a mewing cat outside?'

'No,' said the aged relative. 'No mewing cat. Why, did you order one?'

'I can't bear mewing cats,' said Everard. 'A mewing cat gets on my nerves.'

That was all about mewing cats for the moment. Tea was dished out, and I had a couple of bits of buttered toast, and so the long day wore on till it was time to dress for dinner. The

Fothergill contingent pushed off, and I was heading in the same direction, when Aunt Dahlia arrested my progress.

'Just a second, Bertie, before you put on your clean dickey,' she said. 'I would like to show you something.'

'And I,' I riposted, 'would like to know what this job is you say you want me to do for you.'

'I'll be coming to that later. This thing I'm going to show you is tied in with it. But first a word from our sponsor. Did you notice anything about Everard Fothergill just now?'

I reviewed the recent past.

'Would you describe him as perhaps a bit jumpy? He seemed to me to be stressing the mewing cat motif rather more strongly than might have been expected.'

'Exactly. He's a nervous wreck. Cornelia tells me he used to be very fond of cats.'

'He still appears interested in them.'

'It's this blasted picture that has sapped his morale.'

'Which blasted picture would that be?'

'I'll show you. Step this way.'

She led me into the dining-room and switched on the light.

'Look,' she said.

What she was drawing to my attention was a large oil painting. A classical picture, I suppose you would have called it. Stout female in the minimum of clothing in conference with a dove.

'Venus?' I said. It's usually a safe bet.

'Yes. Old Fothergill painted it. He's just the sort of man who would paint a picture of Ladies Night In A Turkish Bath and call it Venus. He gave it to Everard as a wedding present.'

'Thus saving money on the customary fish-slice. Shrewd, very shrewd. And I gather from what you were saying that the latter does not like it.'

'Of course he doesn't. It's a mess. The old boy's just an incompetent amateur. But being devoted to his father and not wanting to hurt his feelings Everard can't have it taken down and put in the cellar. He's stuck with it, and has to sit looking at it every time he puts on the nosebag. With what result?'

'The food turns to ashes in his mouth?'

'Exactly. It's driving him potty. Everard's a real artist. His stuff's good. Some of it's in the Tate. Look at this,' she said, indicating another canvas. 'That's one of his things.'

I gave it a quick once-over. It, too, was a classical picture, and seemed to my untutored mind very like the other one, but presuming that some sort of art criticism was expected of me I said:

'I like the patina.'

That, too, is generally a safe bet, but it appeared that I had said the wrong thing, for the relative snorted audibly.

'No, you don't, you miserable blighter. You don't even know what a patina is.'

She had me there, of course. I didn't.

'You and your ruddy patinas! Well, anyway, you see why Everard has got the jitters. If a man can paint as well as he can, it naturally cuts him to the quick to have to glue his eyes on a daub like the Venus every time he sits down to break bread. Suppose you were a great musician. Would you like to have to listen to a cheap, vulgar tune – the same tune – day after day? Or suppose that every time you went to lunch at the Drones you had to sit opposite someone who looked like the Hunchback of Notre Dame? Would you enjoy that? Of course you wouldn't. You'd be as sick as mud.'

I saw her point. Many a time at the Drones I have had to sit opposite Oofy Prosser, and it had always taken the edge off a usually keen appetite.

'So now do you grasp the position of affairs, dumb-bell?'

'Oh, I grasp it all right, and the heart bleeds, of course. But I don't see there's anything to be done about it.'

'I do. Ask me what.'

'What?'

'You're going to pinch that Venus.'

I looked at her with a wild surmise, silent upon a peak in Darien. Not my own. One of Jeeves's things.

'Pinch it?'

'This very night.'

'When you say "pinch it", do you mean "*pinch it*"?'

'That's right. That's the little something I was speaking of, the simple little thing you're going to do to help Auntie. Good heavens,' she said, her manner betraying impatience, 'I can't see why you're looking like a stuck pig about it. It's right up your street. You're always pinching policemen's helmets, aren't you?'

I had to correct this.

'Not always. Only as an occasional treat, as it might be on a Boat Race night. And, anyway, pinching pictures is a very different thing from lifting the headgear of the Force. Much more complex.'

'There's nothing complex about it. It's as easy as falling off a log. You just cut it out of the frame with a good sharp knife.'

'I haven't got a good sharp knife.'

'You will have. You know, Bertie,' she said, all enthusiasm, 'it's extraordinary how things fit in. These last weeks there's been a gang of picture-thieves operating in this neighbourhood. They got away with a Romney at a house near here and a Gainsborough from another house. It was that that gave me the idea. When his Venus disappears, there won't be a chance of old Fothergill suspecting anything and having his feelings hurt.

These marauders are connoisseurs, he'll say to himself, only the best is good enough for them. Cornelia agreed with me.'

'You told her?'

'Well, naturally. I was naming the Price of the Papers. I said that if she gave me her solemn word that she would let the *Boudoir* have this slush she's writing, shaving her price to suit my purse, you would liquidate the Edward Fothergill Venus.'

'You did, did you? And what did she say?'

'She thanked me brokenly, saying it was the only way of keeping Everard from going off his rocker, and I told her I would have you here, ready to the last button, this week-end.'

'God bless your old pea-pickin' heart!'

'So go to it, boy, and heaven speed your efforts. All you have to do is open one of the windows, to make it look like an outside job, collect the picture, take it back to your room and burn it. I'll see that you have a good fire.'

'Oh, thanks.'

'And now you had better be dressing. You haven't much time, and it makes Everard nervous if people are late for dinner.'

It was with bowed head and the feeling that the curse had come upon me that I proceeded to my room. Jeeves was there, studding the shirt, and I lost no time in giving him the low-down. My attitude towards Jeeves on these occasions is always that of a lost sheep getting together with its shepherd.

'Jeeves,' I said, 'you remember me telling you in the car that I was weighed down with a nameless foreboding?'

'Yes, sir.'

'Well, I had every right to be. Let me tell you in a few simple words what Aunt Dahlia has just been springing on me.'

I told him in a few simple words, and his left eyebrow rose perhaps an eighth of an inch, showing how deeply he was stirred.

'Very disturbing, sir.'

'Most. And the ghastly thing is that I suppose I shall have to do it.'

'I fear so, sir. Taking into consideration the probability that, should you decline to co-operate, Mrs Travers will place sanctions on you in the matter of Anatole's cooking, you would appear to have no option but to fall in with her wishes. Are you in pain, sir?' he asked, observing me writhe.

'No, just chafing. This has shocked me, Jeeves. I wouldn't have thought such an idea would ever have occurred to her. One could understand Professor Moriarty, and possibly Doctor Fu Manchu, thinking along these lines, but not a wife and mother highly respected in Market Snodsbury, Worcestershire.'

'The female of the species is more deadly than the male, sir. May I ask if you have formulated a plan of action?'

'She sketched one out. I open a window, to make it look like an outside job—'

'Pardon me for interrupting, sir, but there I think Mrs Travers is in error. A broken window would lend greater verisimilitude.'

'Wouldn't it rouse the house?'

'No, sir, it can be done quite noiselessly by smearing treacle on a sheet of brown paper, attaching the paper to the pane and striking it a sharp blow with the fist. This is the recognized method in vogue in the burgling industry.'

'But where's the brown paper? Where the treacle?'

'I can procure them, sir, and I shall be happy to perform the operation for you, if you wish.'

'You will? That's very white of you, Jeeves.'

'Not at all, sir. It is my aim to give satisfaction. Excuse me, I think I hear someone knocking.'

He went to the door, opened it, said 'Certainly, madam, I will give it to Mr Wooster immediately,' and came back with a sort of young sabre.

'Your knife, sir.'

'Thank you, Jeeves, curse it,' I said, regarding the object with a shudder, and slipped sombrely into the mesh-knit underwear.

After deliberation, we had pencilled in the kick-off for one in the morning, when the household might be expected to be getting its eight hours, and at one on the dot Jeeves shimmered in.

'Everything is in readiness, sir.'

'The treacle?'

'Yes, sir.'

'The brown p.?'

'Yes, sir.'

'Then just bust the window, would you mind.'

'I have already done so, sir.'

'You have? Well, you were right about it being noiseless. I didn't hear a sound. Then Ho for the dining-room, I suppose. No sense in dillying or, for the matter of that, dallying.'

'No, sir. If it were done when 'tis done, then 'twere well it were done quickly,' he said, and I remember thinking how neatly he puts these things.

It would be idle to pretend that, as I made my way down the stairs, I was my usual debonair self. The feet were cold, and if there had been any sudden noises, I would have started at them. My meditations on Aunt Dahlia, who had let me in for this horror in the night, were rather markedly lacking in a nephew's love. Indeed, it is not too much to say that every step I took deepened my conviction that what the aged relative needed was a swift kick in the pants.

However, in one respect you had to hand it to her. She had said the removal of the picture from the parent frame would be as easy as falling off a log – a thing I have never done myself, but one which, I should imagine, is reasonably simple of accomplishment – and so it proved. She had in no way overestimated the goodness and sharpness of the knife with which she had provided me. Four quick cuts, and the canvas came out like a winkle at the end of a pin. I rolled it up and streaked back to my room with it.

Jeeves in my absence had been stoking the fire, and it was now in a cheerful blaze. I was about to feed Edward Fothergill's regrettable product to the flames and push it home with the poker, but he stayed my hand.

'It would be injudicious to burn so large an object in one piece, sir. There is the risk of setting the chimney on fire.'

'Ah, yes, I see what you mean. Snip it up, you think?'

'I fear it is unavoidable, sir. Might I suggest that it would relieve the monotony of the task if I were to provide whisky and a syphon?'

'You know where they keep it?'

'Yes, sir.'

'Then lead it to me.'

'Very good, sir.'

'And meanwhile I'll be getting on with the job.'

I did so, and was making good progress, when the door opened without my hearing it and Aunt Dahlia beetled in. She spoke before I was aware of her presence in my midst, causing me to shoot up to the ceiling with a stifled cry.

'Everything pretty smooth, Bertie?'

'I wish you'd toot your horn,' I said, coming back to earth and speaking with not a little bitterness. 'You shook me to the core. Yes, matters have gone according to plan. But Jeeves insists on burning the *corpus delicti* bit by bit.'

'Well, of course. You don't want to set the chimney on fire.'

'That was what he said.'

'And he was right, as always. I've brought my scissors. Where is Jeeves, by the way? Why not at your side, giving selfless service?'

'Because he's giving selfless service elsewhere. He went off to get whisky.'

'What a man! There is none like him, none. Bless my soul,' said the relative some moments later, as we sat before the fire and snipped, 'how this brings back memories of the dear old school and our girlish cocoa parties. Happy days, happy days! Ah, Jeeves, come right in and put the supplies well within my reach. We're getting on, you see. What is that you have hanging on your arm?'

'The garden shears, madam. I am anxious to lend all the assistance that is within my power.'

'Then start lending. Edward Fothergill's masterpiece awaits you.'

With the three of us sparing no effort, we soon completed the work in hand. I had scarcely got through my first whisky and s. and was beginning on another, when all that was left of the Venus, not counting the ashes, was the little bit at the south-east end which Jeeves was holding. He was regarding it with what seemed to me a rather thoughtful eye.

'Excuse me, madam,' he said. 'Did I understand you to say that Mr Fothergill senior's name was Edward?'

'That's right. Think of him as Eddie, if you wish. Why?'

'It is merely that the picture we have with us appears to be signed "Everard Fothergill", madam. I thought I should mention it.'

To say that aunt and nephew did not take this big would be paltering with the truth. We skipped like the high hills.

'Give me that fragment, Jeeves. It looks like Edward to me,' I pronounced, having scrutinized it.

'You're crazy,' said Aunt Dahlia, feverishly wrenching it from my grasp. 'It's Everard. Isn't it, Jeeves?'

'That was certainly the impression I formed, madam.'

'Bertie,' said Aunt Dahlia, speaking in a voice of the kind which I believe is usually called strangled and directing at me the sort of look which in the days when she used to hunt with the Quorn and occasionally the Pytchley she would have given a hound engaged in chasing a rabbit, 'Bertie, you curse of the civilized world, if you've burned the wrong picture...'

'Of course I haven't,' I replied stoutly. 'You're both cockeyed. But if it will ease your mind, I'll pop down to the dining-room and take a dekko. Amuse yourselves somehow till my return.'

I had spoken, as I say, stoutly, and hearing me you would no doubt have said to yourself 'All is well with Bertram. He is unperturbed.' But I wasn't. I feared the worst, and already I was wincing at the thought of the impassioned speech, touching on my mental and moral defects, which Aunt Dahlia would be delivering when we forgathered once more. Far less provocation in the past had frequently led her to model her attitude toward me on that of a sergeant dissatisfied with the porting and shouldering arms of a recruit who had not quite got the hang of the thing.

I was consequently in no vein for the receipt of another shock, but I got this when I reached journey's end, for as I entered the dining-room somebody inside it came bounding out and rammed me between wind and water. We staggered into the hall, locked in a close embrace, and as I had switched on the lights there in order to avoid bumping into pieces of furniture I was enabled to see my dance partner steadily and see him whole, as Jeeves says. It was Fothergill senior in bedroom slippers and a dressing-gown. In his right hand he had a knife, and at his feet there was a bundle of some sort which he had dropped at the moment of impact, and when I picked it up in my courteous way and it came unrolled, what I saw brought a startled 'Golly!' to my lips. It deadheated with a yip of anguish from his. He had paled beneath his whiskers.

'Mr Wooster!' he . . . quavered is, I think, the word. 'Thank God you are not Everard!'

Well, I was pretty pleased about that, too, of course. The last thing I would have wanted to be was a small, thin artist with a beard.

'No doubt,' he proceeded, still quavering, 'you are surprised to find me removing my Venus by stealth in this way, but I can explain everything.'

'Well, that's fine, isn't it?'

'You are not an artist—'

'No, more a literary man. I once wrote an article on What The Well-Dressed Man Is Wearing for *Milady's Boudoir*.'

'Nevertheless, I think I can make you understand what this picture means to me. It was my child. I watched it grow. I loved it. It was part of my life.'

Here he paused, seeming touched in the wind, and I threw in a 'Very creditable' to keep the conversation going.

'And then Everard married, and in a mad moment I gave it to him as a wedding present. How bitterly I regretted it! But the thing was done. It was irrevocable. I saw how he valued the picture. His eyes at meal times were always riveted on it. I could not bring myself to ask him for it back. And yet I was lost without it.'

'Bit of a mix-up,' I agreed. 'Difficult to find a formula.'

'For a while it seemed impossible. And then there was this outbreak of picture robberies in the neighbourhood. You heard about those?'

'Yes, Aunt Dahlia mentioned them.'

'Several valuable paintings have been stolen from houses near here, and it suddenly occurred to me that if I were to – er – remove my Venus, Everard would assume that it was the work of the same gang and never suspect. I wrestled with the temptation ... I beg your pardon?'

'I only said "At-a-boy!".'

'Oh? Well, as I say, I did my utmost to resist the temptation, but tonight I yielded. Mr Wooster, you have a kind face.'

For an instant I thought he had said 'kind of face' and drew myself up, a little piqued. Then I got him.

'Nice of you to say so.'

'Yes, I am sure you are kind and would not betray me. You will not tell Everard?'

'Of course not, if you don't want me to. Sealed lips, you suggest?'

'Precisely.'

'Right ho.'

'Thank you, thank you. I am infinitely grateful. Well, it is a little late and one might as well be turning in, I suppose, so I will say good-night,' he said, and having done so, buzzed up the stairs like a homing rabbit. And scarcely had he buzzed, when I found Aunt Dahlia and Jeeves at my side.

'Oh, there you are,' I said.

'Yes, here we are,' replied the relative with a touch of asperity. 'What's kept you all this time?'

'I would have made it snappier, but I was somewhat impeded in my movements by pards.'

'By what?'

'Bearded pards. Shakespeare. Right, Jeeves?'

'Perfectly correct, sir. Shakespeare speaks of the soldier as bearded like the pard.'

'And,' said Aunt Dahlia, 'full of strange oaths. Some of which you will shortly hear, if you don't tell us what you're babbling about.'

'Oh, didn't I mention that? I've been chatting with Edward Fothergill.'

'Bertie, you're blotto.'

'Not blotto, old flesh and blood, but much shaken. Aunt Dahlia, I have an amazing story to relate.'

I related my amazing story.

'And so,' I concluded, 'we learn once again the lesson never, however dark the outlook, to despair. The storm clouds lowered, the skies were black, but now what do we see? The sun shining and the blue bird back once more at the old stand. La Fothergill wanted the Venus expunged, and it has been expunged. Voilà!' I said, becoming a bit Parisian.

'And when she finds that owing to your fatheadedness Everard's very valuable picture has also been expunged?'

I h'med. I saw what she had in mind.

'Yes, there's that,' I agreed.

'She'll be madder than a wet hen. There isn't a chance now that she'll let me have that serial.'

'I'm afraid not. I had overlooked that. I withdraw what I said about the sun and the blue bird.'

She inflated her lungs, and it could have been perceived by the dullest eye that she was about to begin.

'Bertie—'

Jeeves coughed that soft cough of his, the one that sounds like a sheep clearing its throat on a distant mountain side.

'I wonder if I might make a suggestion, madam?'

'Yes, Jeeves? Remind me,' said the relative, giving me a burning glance, 'to go on with what I was saying later. You have the floor, Jeeves.'

'Thank you, madam. It was merely that it occurs to me as a passing thought that there is a solution of the difficulty that confronts us. If Mr Wooster were to be found here lying stunned, the window broken and both pictures removed, Mrs Fothergill could, I think, readily be persuaded that he found miscreants making a burglarious entry and while endeavouring to protect her property was assaulted and overcome by them. She would, one feels, be grateful.'

Aunt Dahlia came up like a rocket from the depths of gloom in which she had been wallowing. Her face, always red owing to hunting in all weathers in her youth, took on a deeper vermilion.

'Jeeves, you've hit it! I see what you mean. She would be so all over him for his plucky conduct that she couldn't decently fail to come through about the serial.'

'Precisely, madam.'

'Thank you, Jeeves.'

'Not at all, madam.'

'When, many years hence, you hand in your dinner pail, you must have your brain pickled and presented to the nation. It's a colossal scheme, don't you think, Bertie?'

I had been listening to the above exchange of remarks without a trace of Aunt Dahlia's enthusiasm, for I had spotted the flaw in the thing right away – to wit, the fact that I was not lying stunned. I now mentioned this.

'Oh, that?' said Aunt Dahlia. 'We can arrange that. I could give you a tap on the head with ... with what, Jeeves?'

'The gong stick suggests itself, madam.'

'That's right, with the gong stick. And there we'll be.'

'Well, good-night, all,' I said. 'I'm turning in.'

She stared at me like an aunt unable to believe her ears.

'You mean you won't play ball?'

'I do.'

'Think well, Bertram Wooster. Reflect what the harvest will be. Not a smell of Anatole's cooking will you get for months and months and months. He will dish up his Sylphides à la crème d'Écrevisses and his Timbales de Ris de Veau Toulousaines and what not, but you will not be there to dig in and get yours. This is official.'

I drew myself to my full height.

'There is no terror, Aunt Dahlia, in your threats, for ... how does it go, Jeeves?'

'For you are armed so strong in honesty, sir, that they pass by you like the idle wind, which you respect not.'

'Exactly. I have been giving considerable thought to this matter of Anatole's cooking, and I have reached the conclusion that the thing is one that cuts both ways. Heaven, of course, to chew his smoked offerings, but what of the waistline? The last time I enjoyed your hospitality for the summer months, I put on a full inch round the middle. I am better without Anatole's cooking. I don't want to look like Uncle George.'

I was alluding to the present Lord Yaxley, a prominent

London clubman who gets more prominent yearly, especially seen sideways.

'So,' I continued, 'agony though it may be, I am prepared to kiss those Timbales of which you speak goodbye, and I, therefore, meet your suggestion of giving me taps on the head with the gong stick with a resolute *nolle prosequi*.'

'That is your last word, is it?'

'It is,' I said, and it was, for as I turned on my heel something struck me a violent blow on the back hair, and I fell like some monarch of the forest beneath the axe of the woodman.

What's that word I'm trying to think of? Begins with a 'c'. Chaotic, that's the one. For some time after that conditions were chaotic. The next thing I remember with any clarity is finding myself in bed with a sort of booming noise going on close by. This, the mists having lifted, I was able to diagnose as Aunt Dahlia talking. Hers is a carrying voice. She used, as I have mentioned, to go in a lot for hunting, and though I have never hunted myself, I understand that the whole essence of the thing is to be able to make yourself heard across three ploughed fields and a spinney.

'Bertie,' she was saying, 'I wish you would listen and not let your attention wander. I've got news that will send you dancing about the house.'

'It will be some little time,' I responded coldly, 'before I go dancing about any ruddy houses. My head—'

'Yes, of course. A little the worse for wear, no doubt. But don't let's go off into side issues, I want to tell you the final score. The dirty work is attributed on all sides to the gang, probably international, which has been lifting pictures in these parts of late. Cornelia Fothergill is lost in admiration of your intrepid behaviour, as Jeeves foresaw she would be, and she's giving me the serial on easy terms. You were right about the blue bird. It's singing.'

'So is my head.'

'I'll bet it is, and as you would say, the heart bleeds. But we all have to make sacrifices at these times. You can't make an omelette without breaking eggs.'

'Your own?'

'No, Jeeves's. He said it in a hushed voice as he stood viewing the remains.'

'He did, did he? Well, I trust in future ... Oh, Jeeves,' I said, as he entered carrying what looked like a cooling drink.

'Sir?'

'This matter of eggs and omelettes. From now on, if you could see your way to cutting out the former and laying off the latter, I should be greatly obliged.'

'Very good, sir,' said the honest fellow. 'I will bear it in mind.'

Among the names on the list of candidates up for election at the Drones Club there appeared, proposed by R. P. Little and seconded by an influential Crumpet, that of

LITTLE, ALGERNON AUBREY

and several of the Eggs, Beans and Piefaces who had gathered about the notice board were viewing it with concern. In every club you will find an austere conservative element that looks askance at the unusual and irregular.

'He can't do that there here,' said an Egg, putting into words the sentiment of this *bloc*. 'Hoy!' he went on, addressing the Crumpet, who had entered as he spoke. 'What about this nominee of Bingo Little's?'

'Yes,' said a Bean. 'He can try as much as he likes to cloud the issue by calling him "Algernon Aubrey", as if he were a brother or cousin or something, but the stark fact remains that the above is his baby. We don't want infants mewling and puking about the Drones.'

'Keep it clean,' urged a Pieface.

'Shakespeare,' explained the Bean.

'Oh, Shakespeare? Sorry. No,' said the Pieface, 'we don't want any bally babies here.'

A grave look came into the Crumpet's face.

'You want this one,' he said. 'You can't afford to do without him. Recent events have convinced Bingo that this offspring of his is a Grade A mascot, and he feels that the club should have the benefit of his services. Having heard his story, I agree with him. This half-portion's knack of doing the right thing at the right time is uncanny. I believe the child is almost human.'

His eloquence was not without its effect. But though some of the malcontents wavered, the Egg remained firm.

'That's all very well, but the question that presents itself is – Where will this stop? What guarantee have we that if we elect this juvenile, Bingo won't start trying to ring in his old nurse or his Uncle Wilberforce, or the proprietor of that children's paper he's editor of – what's his name – Purkiss?'

'I don't know about the nurse or his Uncle Wilberforce,' said the Crumpet, 'but you need have no anxiety concerning Henry Cuthbert Purkiss. Bingo's relations with his overlord are at the moment formal, even distant. Owing to Purkiss, he recently had to undergo a mental strain almost without parallel in his experience. And though, thanks to this beneficent baby's faultless sense of timing, he was enabled to emerge from the soup which was lashing angrily about his ankles, he finds it difficult to forgive. He expressly stated to me that if Henry Cuthbert Purkiss were to step on a banana skin and strain a ligament, it would be all right with him.'

'What did Purkiss do?'

'It was what he didn't do. He refused to pay ten quid for Bingo's story, and this at a crisis in Bingo's affairs when only ten quid could save him from the fate that is worse than death – viz. having the wife of his bosom draw in her breath sharply and look squiggle-eyed at him. He had been relying on Purkiss to do the square thing, and Purkiss let him down.'

*   *   *

Here briefly (said the Crumpet) are the facts. As most of you are probably aware, Bingo buzzed off a couple of years ago and went and married the eminent female novelist Rosie M. Banks, authoress of *Only A Factory Girl*, *Mervyn Keene, Clubman*, *'Twas Once in May* and other stearine works of fiction, and came a day when there burst on the London scene a bouncing baby of the name of Algernon Aubrey. Very pleasant for all concerned, of course, but the catch is that this sort of thing puts ideas in the heads of female novelists. As they sat at dinner one night, Mrs Bingo looked up from her portion of steak and French fried, and said:

'Oh, sweetie-pie,' for it is thus that she habitually addresses the other half of the sketch, 'you haven't forgotten it's Algy's birthday on the twenty-third? Just think! He'll be one year old.'

'Pretty senile, pretty senile,' said Bingo. 'Silver threads among the gold, what? We must give him a rattle or something.'

'We can do better than rattles. Shall I tell you the wonderful thing I've thought of?'

'Say on, old partner in sickness and in health.'

And Mrs Bingo said that she had decided to start a wee little deposit account for Algernon Aubrey at the local bank. She was going to pay in ten pounds, and her mother was going to pay in ten pounds, and so was the child's maternal aunt Isabel, and what a lovely surprise it would be for the young buster, when he got older, to find that all unknown his dear ones had been working on his behalf, bumping up his holdings like billy-o. And Bingo, mellowed by a father's love, got the party spirit and said that if that was the trend affairs were taking, blow him tight if he didn't chip in and add to the kitty his own personal tenner.

Upon which, Mrs Bingo said: 'Oh, sweet-ie-*pie*!' And kissed him with a good deal of fervour, and the curtain of Act One falls on a happy and united home.

Now, though at the moment when he made this fine gesture Bingo actually had ten quid in his possession, having touched Purkiss for an advance on his salary, one would have expected him, thinking things over in the cold grey light of the morning after, to kick himself soundly for having been such an ass as to utter those unguarded words, committing him as they did to a course of conduct which would strip him of his last bean. But such was not the case. Still mellowed by a father's love, all he thought next day was that as a gift to a superchild like Algernon Aubrey a tenner was a bit on the cheese-paring side. Surely twenty would be far more suitable. And he could pick that up by slapping his ten on Hot Potato in the two-thirty at Haydock Park. At dinner on the previous night he had burned his mouth by incautiously placing in it a fried spud about ninety degrees Fahrenheit warmer than he had supposed it to be, and he is always far too inclined to accept omens like this as stable information. He made the investment, accordingly, and at two-forty-five was informed by the club tape that he was now penniless.

Well, as you can readily imagine, it did not take him long to perceive that a crisis of the first magnitude had been precipitated. Mrs Bingo, a charming woman but deficient in sporting blood, had strictly forbidden him ever to venture money on the speed and endurance of racehorses, and the discovery that he had once more been chancing his arm would be bound to lead to an unpleasant scene, from which he shrank. As every young husband knows, there is nothing less agreeable than having the little woman bring her teeth together with a sharp click and after saying 'Oh, how *could* you?' follow it up with about two thousand words of the kind that go through the soul like a bullet through butter.

And discovery, unless he could somehow balance the budget, was of course inevitable. Sooner or later Mrs Bingo would be taking a look at the infant's wee little passbook, and when she did would immediately spot something wrong with the wee little figures. 'Hoy!' she would cry. 'Where's that ten-spot you said you were depositing?' and from this to the bleak show-down would be but a short step.

It was a situation in which many fellows would just have turned their faces to the wall and waited for the end. But there is good stuff in Bingo. A sudden inspiration showed him the way out. He sat right down and wrote a story about a little girl called Gwendoline and her cat Tibby. The idea of course being to publish it in *Wee Tots* and clean up.

It was no easy task. Until he started on it he had had no notion what blood, sweat and tears are demanded from the poor sap who takes a pop at the life literary, and a new admiration for Mrs Bingo awoke in him. Mrs Bingo, he knew, did her three thousand words a day without ricking a muscle, and to complete this Tibby number, though it ran only to about fifteen hundred, took him over a week, during which period he on several occasions as near as a toucher went off his onion.

However, he finished it at last, copied it out neatly, submitted it to himself, read it with considerable interest and accepted it, putting it down on the charge sheet for ten of the best. And when pay day arrived and no tenner, he sought audience of Purkiss.

'Oh, Mr Purkiss,' he said. 'Sorry to come butting in at a moment when you were probably meditating, but it's about that story.'

Purkiss looked at him fishily. Nature having made it impossible for him to look at anyone otherwise, he being a man with a face like a halibut.

'Story?'

Bingo explained the circumstances. He said that he was the author of 'Tibby's Wonderful Adventure' in the current issue, and Purkiss Oh-yes-ed and said he had read it with considerable interest, and Bingo oh-thanks-ed and simpered coyly, and then there was a rather long silence.

'Well, how about the emolument?' said Bingo at length, getting down to the *res*.

Purkiss started. The fishy glitter in his eye became intensified. He looked like a halibut which has just been asked by another halibut to lend it a couple of quid till next Wednesday.

'There should be a tenner coming to me,' said Bingo.

'Oh, no, no, no,' said Purkiss. 'Oh, no, no, no, no, no. All contributions which you may make to the paper are of course covered by your salary.'

'What!' cried Bingo. 'You mean I don't touch?'

Purkiss assured him that he did not, and Bingo tottered from the room and went off to the club to pull himself together with a couple of quick ones. And he was just finishing the second when Oofy Prosser came in. One glance at him told Bingo that here was the fountainhead to which he must go. He needed someone to lend him a tenner, and Oofy, he felt, was the People's Choice.

Now I need scarcely tell you that a fellow who is going to lend you a tenner must have two prime qualifications. He must be good for the amount and he must be willing to part with it. Oofy unquestionably filled the bill in the first particular, but experience had taught Bingo that he was apt to fall down on the second. Nevertheless it was in optimistic mood that he beetled over to his old friend. Oofy, he reminded himself, was Algernon Aubrey's godfather, and it was only natural to suppose that he would be delighted to come through with a birthday present for the little chap. Well, not delighted, perhaps. Still, a bit of persevering excavating work would probably dig up the needful.

'Oh, hullo, Oofy, old man,' he said. 'Oofy, old man, do you know what? It's Algy's birthday very shortly.'

'Algy who?'

'Algy A. Little. The good old baby. Your godson.'

A quick shudder ran through Oofy. He was thinking of the occasion when he had had a severe morning head and Bingo had brought the stripling to his flat and introduced them.

'Oh, my Aunt!' he said. 'That frightful little gumboil!'

His tone was not encouraging, but Bingo carried on.

'Presents are now pouring in, and I knew you would be hurt if you were not given the opportunity of contributing some little trifle. Ten quid was what suggested itself to me. The simplest thing,' said Bingo, 'would be if you were to slip me the money now. Then it would be off your mind.'

Oofy flushed darkly beneath his pimples.

'Now listen,' he said, and there was no mistaking the ring of determination in his voice. 'When you talked me – against my better judgment – into becoming godfather to a child who looks like a ventriloquist's dummy, I expressly stipulated that a silver mug was to be accepted in full settlement, and we had a gentleman's agreement to that effect. It still holds good.'

'Ten quid isn't much.'

'It's ten quid more than you're going to get out of me.'

Bingo was reluctantly compelled to come clean.

'As a matter of fact, Oofy, old man, it's not the baby who wants the stuff, it's me – your old friend, the fellow you've known since he was so high. Unless I get a tenner immediately, disaster stares me in the eyeball. So give of your plenty, Oofy, like the splendid chap you are.'

'No!' cried Oofy. 'No, no, a thousand times—'

The words died on his lips. It was as though a thought had come, flushing his brow.

'Listen,' he said. 'Are you doing anything this evening?'

'No. Unless I decide to end it all in the river.'

'Can you slip away from home?'

'Yes, I could do that all right. As it happens, I'm all alone at the moment. My wife and Mrs Purkiss, the moon of my boss's delight, have legged it to Brighton to attend some sort of Old Girls binge at their late school, and won't be back till tomorrow.'

'Good. I want you to dine at the Ritz.'

'Fine. Nothing I should like better. I meet you there, do I?'

'You do not. I'm leaving for Paris this afternoon. What you meet is a girl named Mabel Murgatroyd with red hair, a vivacious manner and a dimple on the left side of the chin. You give her dinner.'

Bingo drew himself up. He was deeply shocked at the other's loose ideas of how married men behave when their wives are away.

'Do this, and you get your tenner.'

Bingo lowered himself.

'Listen,' said Oofy. 'I will tell you all.'

It was a dubious and discreditable story that he related. For some time past, it appeared, he had been flitting round this girl like a pimpled butterfly, and it had suddenly come to him with a sickening shock that his emotional nature had brought him to the very verge of matrimony. Another step and he would be over the precipice. It was the dimple that did it principally, he said. Confronted with it at short range, he tended to say things which in sober retrospect he regretted.

'I asked her to dine with me tonight,' he concluded, 'and if I go, I'm sunk. Only instant flight can save me. But that's not all. I want you not only to give her dinner, but finally and definitely to choke her off me. You must roast me roundly. Pretend you think I'm the world's leading louse.'

The verb 'pretend' did not seem to Bingo very happily chosen, but he nodded intelligently.

'Here's your tenner,' said Oofy, 'and here's the money for the dinner. Don't get carried away by that dimple and forget to roast me.'

'I won't.'

'Pitch it strong. I'll tell you some things to say.'

'No, no, don't bother,' said Bingo. 'I'll think of them.'

Bingo had not been waiting long in the lobby of the Ritz that night when a girl appeared, so vermilion in the upper storey and so dimpled on the left side of the chin that he had no hesitation in ambling up and establishing contact.

'Miss Murgatroyd?'

'You never spoke a truer word.'

'My name is Little, R. P. Oofy Prosser, having been unexpectedly called away to the Continent, asked me to roll up and deputize for him.'

'Well, I must say it's a bit thick, asking a girl to dinner and then buzzing off to Continents.'

'Not for Oofy,' said Bingo, starting the treatment. 'His work is generally infinitely thicker than that. I don't know how well you know him?'

'Fairly well.'

'When you know him really well you will realize that you are up against something quite exceptional. Take a wart hog, add a few slugs and some of those things you see under flat stones, sprinkle liberally with pimples, and you will have something which, while of course less loathsome than Alexander Prosser, will give you the general idea.'

And so saying, he led her into the dining salon and the meal started.

It went with a swing from start to finish. The girl's views on Oofy proved to be as sound as his own. She told him that she had gone around with this Prosser because he had made such a point of it, but, left to herself, she would not have touched him with a ten-foot pole. And as Bingo would not willingly have touched Oofy with an eleven-foot pole, a perfect harmony prevailed.

It was some two hours later that the girl rose.

'Oh, don't go yet,' pleaded Bingo, for it seemed to him that they had not nearly exhausted the topic of Oofy, but she was firm.

'I must,' she said. 'I promised to meet a man I know at one of these private gambling places.'

The words stirred Bingo like a bugle. He had heard much of these establishments, but had never had the opportunity of visiting one, and the tenner Oofy had given him seemed to leap in his pocket. Technically, of course, it belonged to Algernon Aubrey, but he knew no son of his would object to him borrowing it for the evening for such a worthy purpose.

'Gosh!' he said. 'You couldn't take me along, could you?'

'Why, of course, if you want to come. It's out in the wilds of St John's Wood somewhere.'

'Really? Then it's on my way home. I live in St John's Wood.'

'I've got the address written down. Forty-three Magnolia Road.'

Bingo, always on the lookout for omens and portents, leaped in his seat. Any lingering doubts he may have entertained as to the advisability of arranging that loan with Algernon Aubrey vanished. Obviously this was going to be his lucky night, and he would be vastly surprised if on the morrow he would not be able to pay twenty or thirty pounds into the other's wee little deposit account.

'Of all the coincidences!' he exclaimed. 'That's next door but one to my little nest.'

The girl said Well, fancy that, adding that it was a small world, and Bingo agreed that he had seldom met a smaller.

The police raid on Number Forty-three Magnolia Road took place, oddly enough, just as Bingo was preparing to leave. He had lost the last of his borrowed capital at the roulette board owing to a mistaken supposition that Red was going to turn up, and was standing at an open window, trying by means of some breaths of fresh air to alleviate that Death-where-is-thy-sting feeling that comes to gamesters at such times, when suddenly bells began to ring all over the place and a number of those present, jostling him to one side, proceeded to pour out of the window in a foaming stream.

Always a quick thinker, it took him but an instant to appreciate that the minds of these persons were working along the right lines. He knew what happened to those who dallied and loitered on occasions like this. They appeared next day before the awful majesty of the Law, charged with being found on enclosed premises, entered by virtue of a warrant in writing signed by the Commissioner of Police and alleged to be a common gaming house, contrary to Section 6 of the Gaming Act of 1845, – the last thing a young husband, whose wife disapproved of gaming houses, would wish to occur.

With the utmost promptitude he added himself to the torrent. A quick dash, and he was in the garden of the house next door to his own, hiding in a convenient water barrel that stood against the potting shed, where some moments later he was joined by Mabel Murgatroyd, who seemed in petulant mood.

'This is the fourth or fifth time this has happened to me,' she said peevishly, as she slid into the barrel's interior. 'Why can't these rozzers have a heart and not be for ever interfering with private enterprise? Do you know what? I had a quid on sixteen, and sixteen came up, but before I could collect the bells began to ring and it was Ho for the open spaces. Thirty-seven pounds sterling gone with the wind. Shift over a bit, will you.'

Bingo shifted over a bit.

'These water barrels are always rather cramped,' he said. 'Still, this one hasn't any water in it,' he added, pointing out the bright side.

'No, there's that, of course. But last time I hid in a cucumber frame. Solid comfort, that was. Ease away, you're crowding me. I wish you wouldn't suddenly expand like that.'

'I was only breathing.'

'Well, don't breathe. Is this your water barrel, by the way?'

'No, I'm just a lodger. What gave you that idea?'

'I thought you told me you lived next door to the recent Casino.'

'Next door but one. We are at the moment enjoying the hospitality of an artist of the name of Quintin.'

'Nice fellow?'

'Not particularly.'

'Ah, well, who is? Hullo, am I wrong, or have things quieted down somewhat? I believe the All Clear's been blown.'

And so it proved. They emerged, paused for a moment on the lawn to take a cordial farewell, and then she went her way and he his. With something of the emotions of one who has been tried in the furnace, he hopped over the fence, sneaked into the house and so to bed.

He slept late next morning, and was about to set out for the office of *Wee Tots*, though feeling ill attuned to the task of providing wholesome reading matter for the juvenile public, when Mrs Bingo came in, back from Brighton.

'Oh, hullo, my precious dream-rabbit,' said Bingo with as much animation as he could dig up. 'Welcome to Meadowsweet Hall. I've missed you, Angel.'

'Me, too, you, sweetie-pie. And I seem to have missed all sorts of excitement. Mrs Simmons across the way was telling me about it. Apparently those people at Number Forty-three have been running one of those gambling places, and last night it was raided by the police.'

'Good heavens!'

'I don't wonder you're shocked. We don't want that sort of thing going on in Magnolia Road.'

'I should say not. Disgraceful.'

'But how curious that you should have heard nothing.'

'I sleep very soundly.'

'You must, because Mrs Simmons says there was a great deal of whistling and shouting going on. I expect Mr Quintin was furious. People were running about his garden half the night, and you know how fussy he is. He complained about Algy crying, and your ukulele and everything. He's always complaining. Are you off to the office?'

'Just leaving.'

'Won't you be very late? I hope Mr Purkiss won't be annoyed.'

'Oh, that's all right. I have a thorough understanding with Purkiss, who knows a good man when he sees one. "Be sure always to get a good night's rest," he has often said to me.'

'You don't look as if you had had a good night's rest. You're a sort of funny yellow colour.'

'Intellectual pallor,' said Bingo, and withdrew.

Arrived at the office, he listlessly tried to bring his mind to bear on the letters which had come in for the Correspondence page ('Uncle Percy's Post-Bag'), but he found it difficult to concentrate. The standard of pure reason reached by the little subscribers who wrote to the editor of *Wee Tots* about their domestic pets was never a high one, but today it seemed to him that either he or they must have got water on the brain. There was one communication about a tortoise called Rupert which, in his opinion, would have served as a passport for its young author to any padded cell in the kingdom.

The only thing that enabled him to win through to closing time was the fact that Purkiss was absent. He had telephoned to say that he was nursing a sick headache. Purkiss at this juncture would have been more than he could have coped with.

It was with a feeling of relief that he started homeward at the end of the long day, and he had just unlatched the front door with his latchkey and was standing his hat on the hatstand, when Mrs Bingo spoke from the drawing-room.

'Will you come here a moment, please, Bingo.'

His heart, already low, sank lower. He had a sensitive ear, and he did not like the timbre of her voice. Usually Mrs Bingo's voice seemed to him like the tinkling of silver bells across a scented meadow at sunset, but now it was on the flat side, and he fancied that he detected in it that metallic note which married men dislike so much.

She was standing in mid-carpet, looking cold and stern. She had a paper of some kind in her hand.

'Bingo,' she said, 'where were you last night?'

Bingo passed a finger round the inside of his collar. His brow was wet with honest sweat. But he told himself that he must be calm ... cool ... nonchalant.

'Last night?' he said, frowning thoughtfully. 'Let me see, that would be the night of June the fifteenth, would it not? H'm. Ha. The night of—'

'I see you have forgotten,' said Mrs Bingo. 'Let me refresh your memory. You were fleeing from the police because they had caught you gambling at Number Forty-three.'

'Who me? You're sure you mean me?'

'Read this,' said Mrs Bingo, and thrust at him the document she was holding.

It was a letter, and ran as follows:—

Picasso Lodge
41 Magnolia Road
St John's Wood
London, N.8

Madam:

While sympathizing with your husband's desire to avoid being arrested by the police for gambling on enclosed premises, I would be glad if you would ask him next time not to take refuge in my water barrel, as he and some unidentified female did last night.

I remain,
Yours faithfully,
Dante Gabriel Quintin.

'Well?' said Mrs Bingo.

Bingo's spine had turned to gelatine. It seemed useless to struggle further. His gallant spirit was broken. And he was about to throw in the towel and confess all, when there was a sound outside like a mighty rushing wind and Algernon Aubrey's nanny came tottering in. Her eyes were wide and glassy, she breathed stertorously, and it was obvious that she was in the grip of some powerful emotion.

'Oh, ma'am!' she cried. 'The baby!'

All the Mother in Mrs Bingo awoke. She forgot Bingo and police and water barrels and everything else. She gasped. Bingo gasped. The nanny was already gasping. A stranger, entering the room, would have supposed himself to have strayed into a convention of asthma patients.

'Is he ill?'

'No, ma'am, but he just said "Cat".'

'Cat?'

'Yes, ma'am, as plain as I'm standing here now. I was showing him his little picture book, and we'd come to the rhinoceros, and he pointed his finger at it and looked up at me and said "Cat".'

A footnote is required here for the benefit of those who are not family men. 'Cat', they are probably feeling, is not such a tremendously brilliant and epigrammatic thing to say. But what made Algernon Aubrey's utterance of the word so sensational was that it was his first shot at saying anything. Up till now he had been one of those strong silent babies, content merely to dribble at the side of the mouth and emit an occasional gurgle. It can readily be understood, therefore, that the effect of this piece of hot news on Mrs Bingo was about the same as that of the arrival of Talkies on the magnates of Hollywood. She left the room as if shot out of a gun. The nanny hurried after her. And Bingo was alone.

His first emotion, of course, was one of stunned awe at having been saved from the scaffold at the eleventh hour, but he soon saw that he had been accorded but a brief respite and that on Mrs Bingo's return he would have to have some good, watertight story in readiness for her: and, try as he might, he could think of nothing that would satisfy her rather exacting taste. He toyed with the idea of saying that he had been in conference with Purkiss last night, discussing matters of office policy, but was forced to dismiss it.

For one thing, Purkiss would never abet his innocent deception. All that Bingo had seen of the man told him that the proprietor of *Wee Tots* was one of those rigidly upright blisters who, though possibly the backbone of England, are no earthly use to a chap in an emergency. Purkiss was the sort of fellow who, if approached on the matter of bumping up a pal's alibi, would stare fishily and say 'Am I to understand, Mr Little, that you are suggesting that I sponsor a lie?'

Besides, Purkiss was at his home nursing a sick headache, which meant that negotiations would have to be conducted over the telephone, and you cannot swing a thing like that by remote control. You want the pleading eye and the little pats on the arm.

No, that was no good, and there appeared nothing to be done except groan hollowly, and he was doing this when the door opened and the maid announced 'Mr and Mrs Purkiss'.

As they entered, Bingo, who was pacing the room with unseeing eyes, knocked over a table with a vase, three photograph frames and a bowl of potpourri on it. It crashed to the floor with a noise like a bursting shell, and Purkiss soared silently to the ceiling. As he returned to position one, Bingo saw that his face was Nile green in colour and that there were dark circles beneath his eyes.

'Ah, Mr Little,' said Purkiss.

'Oh, hullo,' said Bingo.

Mrs Purkiss did not speak. She seemed to be brooding on something.

Purkiss proceeded. He winced as he spoke, as if articulation hurt him.

'We are not disturbing you, I hope, Mr Little?'

'Not at all,' said Bingo courteously. 'But I thought you were at home with a sick headache.'

'I was at home with a sick headache,' said Purkiss, 'the result, I think, of sitting in a draught and contracting some form of tic or migraine. But my wife was anxious that you should confirm my statement that I was in your company last night. You have not forgotten that we sat up till a late hour at my club? No doubt you will recall that we were both surprised when we looked at our watches and found how the time had gone?'

There came to Bingo, listening to these words, the illusion that a hidden orchestra had begun to play soft music, while somewhere in the room he seemed to smell the scent of violets and mignonette. His eye, which had been duller than that of Purkiss, suddenly began to sparkle, and what he had supposed to be a piece of spaghetti in the neighbourhood of his back revealed itself as a spine, and a good spine, too.

'Yes,' he said, drawing a deep breath, 'that's right. We were at your club.'

'How the time flew!'

'Didn't it! But then, of course, we were carried away by the topics we were discussing.'

'Quite. We were deep in a discussion of office policy.'

'Absorbing subject.'

'Intensely gripping.'

'You said so-and-so, and I said such-and-such.'

'Precisely.'

'One of the points that came up,' said Bingo, 'was, if you recollect, the question of payment for that story of mine.'

'Was it?' said Purkiss doubtfully.

'Surely you haven't forgotten that?' said Bingo. 'You told me you had been thinking it over and were now prepared to pay me ten quid for it. Or,' he went on, his gaze fixed on the other with a peculiar intensity, 'am I wrong?'

'No, no. It all comes back to me.'

'I may as well take it now,' said Bingo. 'Save a lot of book-keeping.'

Purkiss groaned, perhaps not quite so hollowly as Bingo had been doing before his entrance, but distinctly hollowly.

'Very well,' he said, and as the money changed hands, Mrs Bingo came in.

'Oh, how do you do, Mr Purkiss,' she said. 'Julia,' she cried, turning to Mrs Purkiss, 'you'll never believe! Algy has just said "Cat".'

It was plain that Mrs Purkiss was deeply moved.

'Cat?'

'Yes, isn't it wonderful! Come on up to the nursery, quick. We may be able to get him to say it again.'

Bingo spoke. He made a strangely dignified figure as he stood there looking rather like King Arthur about to reproach Guinevere.

'I wonder, Rosie, if I might have a moment of your valuable time?'

'Well?'

'I shall not detain you long. I merely wish to say what I was about to say just now when you dashed off like a Jack rabbit of the western prairies. If you ask Mr Purkiss, he will tell you that, so far from eluding the constabulary by hiding in water barrels, I was closeted with him at his club till an advanced hour. We were discussing certain problems of interest which had arisen in connection with the conduct of *Wee Tots*. For Mr Purkiss and I are not clockwatchers. We put in overtime. We work while others sleep!'

There was a long silence. Mrs Bingo seemed to sag at the knees, as if some unseen hand had goosed her. Tears welled up in her eyes. Remorse was written on every feature.

'Oh, Bingo!'

'I thought I would just mention it.'

'Oh, sweetie-pie, what can I say? I'm sorry.'

'Quite all right, quite all right. I am not angry. Merely a little hurt.'

Mrs Bingo flung herself into his arms.

'I'm going to sue Mr Quintin for libel!'

'Oh, I wouldn't bother to do that. Just treat him with silent contempt. I doubt if you would get as much as a tenner out of a man like that. Oh, by the way, talking of tenners, here is the one I have been meaning to pay in to Algy's account. You had better take it. I keep forgetting these things. Overwork at the office, no doubt. But I must not detain you, Mrs Purkiss. You will be wishing to go to the nursery.'

Mrs Bingo and Mrs Purkiss passed from the room. Bingo turned to Purkiss, and his eye was stern.

'Purkiss,' he said, 'where *were* you on the night of June the fifteenth?'

'I was with you,' said Purkiss. 'Where were you?'

'I was with you,' said Bingo, 'and a most entertaining companion you were, if you will allow me to say so. But come, let us go and listen to Algernon Aubrey on the subject of Cats. They tell me he is well worth hearing.'

In a corner of the bar parlour of the Angler's Rest a rather heated dispute had arisen between a Small Bass and a Light Lager. Their voices rose angrily.

'Old,' said the Small Bass.

'Ol',' said the Light Lager.

'Bet you a million pounds it's Old.'

'Bet you a million trillion pounds it's Ol'.'

Mr Mulliner looked up indulgently from his hot Scotch and lemon. On occasions like this he is usually called in to arbitrate.

'What is the argument, gentlemen?'

'It's about that song Old Man River,' said the Small Bass.

'Ol' Man River,' insisted the Light Lager. 'He says it's Old Man River, I say it's Ol' Man River. Who's right?'

'In my opinion,' said Mr Mulliner, 'both of you. Mr Oscar Hammerstein, who wrote that best of all lyrics, preferred Ol', but I believe the two readings are considered equally correct. My nephew sometimes employed one, sometimes the other, according to the whim of the moment.'

'Which nephew was that?'

'Reginald, the son of my late brother. He sang the song repeatedly, and at the time of that sudden change in his fortunes was billed to render it at the annual village concert at

Lower-Smattering-on-the-Wissel in Worcestershire, where he maintained a modest establishment.'

'His fortunes changed, did they?'

'Quite remarkably. He was rehearsing the number in an undertone over the breakfast eggs and bacon one morning, when he heard the postman's knock and went to the door.

'Oh, hullo, Bagshot,' he said. 'Shift that trunk.'

'Sir?'

'Lift that bale.'

'To what bale do you refer, sir?'

'Get a little drunk and you ... Oh, sorry,' said Reginald, 'I was thinking of something else. Forget I spoke. Is that a letter for me?'

'Yes, sir. Registered.'

Reginald signed for the letter and, turning it over, saw that the name and address on the back of the envelope were those of Watson, Watson, Watson, Watson and Watson of Lincoln's Inn Fields. He opened it, and found within a communication requesting him to call on the gang at his earliest convenience, when he would hear of something to his advantage.

Something to his advantage being always what he was glad to hear of, he took train to London, called at Lincoln's Inn Fields, and you could have knocked him down with a toothpick when Watson – or Watson or Watson or Watson, or it may have been Watson – informed him that under the will of a cousin in the Argentine, whom he had not seen for years, he had benefited to the extent of fifty thousand pounds. It is not surprising that on receipt of this news he reeled and would have fallen, had he not clutched at a passing Watson. It was enough to stagger anyone, especially someone who, like Reginald, had never been strong in the head. Apart from his ability to sing Old Man River, probably instinctive, he was not a very gifted young man. Amanda Biffen, the girl he loved, though she admired his looks – for, like all the Mulliners, he was extraordinarily handsome – had never wavered in her view that if men were dominoes, he would have been the double blank.

His first act on leaving the Watson office was, of course, to put in a trunk call to Lower Smattering and tell Amanda of this signal bit of luck that had befallen him, for it was going to make all the difference to their love lives. Theirs till now had had to be a secret engagement, neither wishing to disturb the peace of mind of Amanda's uncle and guardian, Sir Jasper Todd, the retired financier. Reginald had one of those nice little bachelor incomes which allow a man to get his three square meals a day and do a certain amount of huntin', shootin' and fishin', but before the descent of these pennies from heaven he had been in no sense a matrimonial prize, and Amanda's theory that Sir Jasper, if informed of the betrothal, would have fifty-seven conniption fits was undoubtedly a correct one.

'Who was that, my dear?' Sir Jasper asked as Amanda came back from the telephone, and Amanda said that it was Reginald Mulliner, speaking from London.

'The most wonderful news. He has been left fifty thousand pounds.'

'He has?' said Sir Jasper. 'Well, well! Just fancy!'

Now when a financier, even a retired one, learns that a young fellow of the mental calibre of Reginald Mulliner has come into possession of fifty thousand pounds, he does not merely say 'Just fancy!' and leave it at that. He withdraws to his study, ties a wet towel about his forehead, has lots of black coffee sent in, and starts to ponder on schemes for getting the stuff away from him.

Sir Jasper had many expenses, and the circumstance of his young friend having acquired this large sum of money seemed to him, for he was a pious man, a direct answer to prayer. He had often felt how bitterly ironical it was that a super-mug like Reginald, so plainly designed by Nature to be chiselled out of his cash, had had no cash to be chiselled out of.

He rang Reginald up at his bungalow a few days later.

'Good morning, Mulliner, my boy.'

'Oh, what ho, Sir Jasper.'

'Amanda . . . I beg your pardon?'

'Eh?'

'I understood you to say "He don't plant taters, he don't plant cotton." Who does not plant potatoes, and how have they and cotton crept into the conversation?'

'Oh, frightfully sorry. I'm singing Old Man River at the village concert tonight, and I must have been rehearsing unconsciously, as it were.'

'I see. A comic song?'

'Well, more poignant, I think you'd call it. Or possibly stark. It's about a negro on the Mississippi who trembles a bit when he sees a job of work.'

'Quite. I believe many negroes do. Well, be that as it may, Amanda has been telling me of your good fortune. My heartiest congratulations. I wonder if you could spare the time to come and see me this morning. I would enjoy a chat.'

'Oh, rather.'

'Don't come immediately, if you don't mind, as I have a man from the insurance company calling in a few minutes about increasing the insurance on my house. Suppose we say an hour from now? Excellent.'

And at the appointed time Reginald alighted from his new

motor-cycle at the door of Sir Jasper's residence, Wissel Hall, and found Sir Jasper on the front steps, bidding farewell to a man in a bowler hat. The bowler-hatted one took his departure, and the financier regarded the motor-cycle with what seemed to Reginald disapproval.

'A recent purchase, is it not?'

'I got it a couple of days ago.'

Sir Jasper shook his head.

'A costly toy. I hope, Mulliner, you are not one of those young men who, when suddenly enriched, get it up their noses and start squandering their substance on frivolities and gew-gaws?'

'Good Lord, no,' said Reginald. 'I plan to freeze on to my little bit of lolly like a porous plaster. The lawyer bloke from whom I heard of something to my advantage was recommending me to put it into a thing called Funding Loan. Don't ask me what it is, because I haven't the foggiest, but it's something run by the Government, and you buy a chunk of it and get back so much twice a year, just like finding it in the street. They pay four and a half per centum per annum, whatever that means, with the net result, according to this legal eagle, that my fifty thousand will bring me in rather more than two thousand a year. Fairly whizzo, I call it, and one wonders how long this has been going on.'

To his surprise, Sir Jasper did not appear to share his enthusiasm. It would be too much, perhaps, to say that he sneered, but he came very close to sneering.

'Two thousand is not much.'

'Oh, isn't it?'

'In these days of inflation and rising costs, a mere pittance. Would you not prefer twenty-five thousand?'

'Yes, that would be nice.'

'Then it can be quite simply arranged. Have you made a study of the oil market?'

'I don't think there is a special market for oil. I get mine at the garage.'

'But you know how vital oil is to our industries?'

'Oh, rather. Sardines and all that.'

'Just so. There is no sounder investment. Now there happens to be among my effects a block of Smelly River Ordinaries, probably the most valuable share on the market, and I think I could let you have fifty thousand pounds' worth of them, as you are – may I say? – a personal friend. They would bring you in a safe fifty per centum.'

'Per annum?'

'Exactly.'

'Per person?'

'Precisely. The annual yield would be, I imagine, somewhere in the neighbourhood of twenty-five or thirty thousand pounds.'

'I say! That sounds smashing! But are you sure you can spare them? Won't you be losing money?'

Sir Jasper smiled.

'When you get to my age, my boy, you will realize that money is not everything in life. As somebody once said, "I expect to pass through this world but once. Any good thing, therefore, that I can do, or any kindness that I can show to a fellow creature, let me do it now, for I shall not pass this way again." Sign here,' said Sir Jasper, producing from an inner pocket a number of stock certificates, a blank cheque, a fountain pen and a piece of blotting paper.

It was with uplifted heart that Reginald went in search of Amanda. He found her, dressed for tennis, about to start off in her car for a neighbouring house, and told her the great news. His income, he said, from now on would be twenty-five thousand pounds or thereabouts each calendar year, which you couldn't say wasn't a bit of a good egg, and this desirable state of things was entirely due to the benevolence of her Uncle Jasper. He had no hesitation, he said, in asking Heaven to bless Sir Jasper Todd.

To his concern, the girl, instead of running about clapping her little hands, shot straight up into the air like a cat which has rashly sat on a too hot radiator.

'You mean to say,' she cried, coming back to earth and fixing him with a burning eye, 'that you gave him the whole fifty thousand?'

'Not "gave", old crumpet,' said Reginald, amused. Women understand so little of finance. 'What happens on these occasions is that one chap, as it might be me, slips another chap, as it might be your uncle, a spot of cash, and in return receives what are called shares. And such shares, for some reason which I haven't quite grasped yet, are the source of wealth beyond the dreams of avarice. These Smelly River Ordinaries, for instance—'

Amanda uttered a snort which ran through the quiet garden like a pistol shot.

'Let me tell you something,' she said, speaking from between clenched teeth. 'One of my earliest recollections as a child is of sitting on Uncle Jasper's knee and listening, round-eyed, while he told me how, at a moment when he was not feeling quite himself, having been hit on the head with a bottle by a disgruntled shareholder at a general meeting, he had allowed some hornswoggling highbinder to stick him with these dud Smelly River Ordinaries. I can still remember the light that shone in his eyes as he spoke of his resolve some day, somewhere, to find a mug on whom he could unload them. He realized that such a mug would have to be the Mug Supreme, the sort of mug that happens only once in a lifetime, but that was the gleam which he was following patiently through the years, never deviating from his purpose, and he was confident of eventual success. He related the story to illustrate what Tennyson had meant when he wrote about rising on stepping stones of our dead selves to higher things.'

It was not easy to depress Reginald Mulliner, but this *conte* had done it. Her words, it seemed to him, could have but one meaning.

'Are you telling me that these ruddy shares are no ruddy good?'

'As wall paper, perhaps, they might lend a tasteful note to a study or rumpus room, but otherwise I should describe their value as non-existent.'

'Well, I'm blowed!'

'You are also bust.'

'Then how are we going to get married?'

'We aren't. I do not propose,' said Amanda coldly, 'to link my lot with that of a man who on the evidence would seem to be a member in good standing of the Jukes family. If you are interested in my future plans, I will sketch them out for you. I am now going off to play tennis with Lord Knubble of Knopp at Knubble Towers. Between the sets or possibly while standing me a gin and tonic at the end of the game he will, I imagine, ask me to be his wife. He always has so far. On this occasion my reply will be in the affirmative. Goodbye, Reginald. It has been nice knowing you. If you follow the path to the right, you will find your way out.'

Reginald was not a quickwitted man, but, reading between the lines, he seemed to sense what she was trying to say.

'This sounds like the raspberry.'

'It is.'

'You mean all is over?'

'I do.'

'You are casting me aside like a ... what are those things people cast aside?'

' "Worn-out glove" is, I presume, the expression for which you are groping.'

'Do you know,' said Reginald, struck by a thought, 'I don't believe I've ever cast aside a worn-out glove. I always give mine to the Salvation Army. However, that is not the point at issue. The point at issue is that you have broken my bally heart.'

'A girl with less self-control,' said Amanda, switching her tennis racquet, 'would have broken your bally head.'

Such then was the situation in which Reginald Mulliner found himself on this sunny summer day, and it was one that seemed to him to present few redeeming features. He was down fifty thousand pounds, he had lost the girl he loved, his heart was broken, and he had a small pimple coming on the back of his neck – a combination which in his opinion gave him a full hand. The only thing that could possibly be regarded as an entry on the credit side was that his spiritual anguish had put him in rare shape for singing Old Man River at the village concert.

Too little attention has been given by our greatest minds to the subject of Old Man River-singing, though such a subject is of absorbing interest. It has never, as far as one knows, been pointed out that this song is virtually impossible of proper rendition by a vocalist who is feeling boomps-a-daisy and on top of the world. The full flavour can be obtained and the last drop of juice squeezed out only by the man who is down among the wines and spirits and brooding gloomily on life in general.

Hamlet would have sung it superbly. So would Schopenhauer and J. B. Priestley. And so, at eight o'clock that night, up on the platform at the village hall with the Union Jack behind him and Miss Frisby, the music teacher, playing the accompaniment at his side, did Reginald Mulliner.

He had not been feeling any too happy to begin with, and the sight of Amanda in the front row in close proximity to a horse-faced young man with large ears and no chin, in whom he recognized Lord Knubble of Knopp, set the seal on his sombre mood, lending to each low note something of the quality of the *obiter dicta* of Hamlet's father's ghost. By the time he had reached that 'He must know somefin', he don't say nuffin', he jest keeps rollin' along' bit there was not a dry eye in the house – or very few – and the applause that broke out from the two-bob seats, the one-bob seats, the sixpenny seats and the threepenny standees at the back can only be described as thunderous. He took three encores and six bows and, had not the curtain been lowered for the inter-mission, might have stolen a seventh. That organ of the theatre world, *Variety*, does not cover amateur concerts at places like Lower-Smattering-on-the-Wissel, but if it did its headline for Reginal Mulliner's performance that night would have been

MULL SWEET SOCKO

The effect on Reginald of this tornado of enthusiasm was rather remarkable. It was as though he had passed through some great spiritual experience which left him a changed man. Nor-mally diffident, he was conscious now of a strange new sense of power. He felt masterful and dominant and for the first time capable of seeking out Sir Jasper Todd, who until now had always overawed him, and telling him just what he thought of him. Before he had even emerged into the open air, six excellent descriptions of Sir Jasper had occurred to him, the mildest of which was 'pot-bellied old swindler'. He resolved to lose no time in sharing these with the financier face to face.

He had not seen Sir Jasper among the audience. In the seat in which he should have been sitting, on Amanda's right, the eye had rested on what looked like a woman of good family who kept cats. The inference, therefore, was that he had given the concert a miss and was having a quiet evening at home, and it was to his home, accordingly, that Reginald now made his way.

Wissel Hall was a vast Tudor mansion, one of those colossal edifices which retired financiers so often buy on settling in the country and the purchase of which, when they realize what it is going to cost to keep them up, they almost invariably regret. Built in the days when a householder thought home was not home unless one had accommodation for sixty guests and a corresponding number of attendant scurvy knaves and varlets, it towered to the skies rather in the manner of Windsor Castle, and in conversation with other retired financiers Sir Jasper usually referred to it as a white elephant and a pain in the neck.

When Reginald reached the massive front door, the fact that repeated ringing of the bell produced no response suggested that the domestic staff had been given the night off to attend the concert. But he was convinced that the man he sought was somewhere inside, and as he had now thought of five more names to call him, bringing the total to eleven, he had no intention of being foiled by a closed front door. As Napoleon would have done in his place, he hunted around till he had found a ladder. Bringing this back and propping it up against the balcony of one of the rooms on the first floor, he climbed up. He had now thought of a twelfth name, and it was the best of the lot.

Windows of country houses are seldom fastened at night, and

he had no difficulty in opening the one outside of which he stood. He found himself in an ornate guest room, and passing through this and down the corridor outside came to a broad gallery looking down on the main hall.

This was at the moment empty, but presently Sir Jasper appeared through a door at the far end. He had presumably been down in the cellar, for he was carrying a large container from which he now proceeded to sprinkle about the floor what from its aroma was evidently paraffin. As he did so, he sang in a soft undertone the hymn which runs 'We plough the fields and scatter the good seed o'er the land.' The floor, Reginald observed, was liberally strewn with paper and shavings.

Odd, he felt. No doubt one of these newfangled methods of removing stains from carpets. Probably very effective, but had their relations been more cordial, he would have shouted down to the financier, warning him that he was running a grave risk of starting a fire. One cannot be too careful with paraffin.

But he was in no mood to give this man kindly warnings. All he wanted to do was start calling him the names, now fourteen in number, which were bubbling in the boiling cauldron of his soul. And he was about to do so, when he chanced to look down at his hand as it rested on the rail, and the sight gave him pause.

I have carelessly omitted to mention – one gets carried away by one's story and tends to overlook small details – that in order to perfect his rendering of Old Man River Reginald had smeared his face and hands with burnt cork. The artist in him had told him that it would be too silly, a chap coming out in faultless evening dress, with a carnation in his buttonhole and a pink face protruding from a high collar, and trying to persuade an intelligent audience that he was an Afro-American in reduced circumstances who wanted to be taken away from the Mississippi.

This, of course, radically altered the run of the scenario. Though, as has been shown, not very intelligent, he could see that a bimbo – call him Bimbo A – who wants to dominate another bimbo – Bimbo B, as it might be – starts at a serious disadvantage if he is blacked up. The wrong note is struck from the outset. It would be necessary, if he was to render so tough an old bounder as Sir Jasper Todd less than the dust beneath his chariot wheels, to go home and wash.

Tut-tutting, for this hitch made him feel frustrated and disappointed, he returned to the ladder and climbed down it. And his foot was leaving the last rung, when a heavy hand descended on his shoulder and a voice, gruesomely official in its intonation, observed 'Ho!' It was Police Constable Popjoy, the sleepless guardian of the peace of Lower-Smattering-On-The-Wissel, who had made this remark. He was one of the few inhabitants of the village who had not attended the concert. Concerts meant nothing to P.C. Popjoy. Duty, stern daughter of the voice of God, told him, concert or no concert, to walk his beat at night, and he walked it.

His task involved keeping an eye on the home of Sir Jasper Todd, and the eye he had been keeping had detected a negroid burglar coming down a ladder from a first-floor balcony. It had struck him from the very first as suspicious. Nice goings-on, thought P.C. Popjoy, and he gripped him, as stated, by the shoulder.

'Ho!' he said again. He was a man of few words, and those mostly of one syllable.

And what, meanwhile, of Amanda?

All through Reginald's deeply moving performance she had sat breathless, her mind in a whirl and her soul stirred to her very depths. With each low note that he pulled up from the soles of his shoes she could feel the old affection and esteem surging back into her with a whoosh, and long before he had taken his sixth bow she knew that he was, if one may coin a phrase, the only onion in the stew and that it would be madness to try to seek happiness elsewhere, particularly as the wife of a man with large ears and no chin, who looked as if he were about to start in the two-thirty race at Kempton Park.

'I love you, I love you!' she murmured, and when Lord Knubble, overhearing the words, beamed and said 'At-a-girl, that's the spirit', she had turned on him with a cold 'Not you, you poor fish', and broken their engagement. And now she was driving home, thinking long, sad thoughts of the man she adored, the man lost to her, she feared, for ever.

Could he ever forgive those harsh words she had spoken?

Extremely doubtful.

Would she ever see him again?

Against this second question one can pencil in the word 'Yes', for at this moment, having freed himself from his custodian's grasp with a shrewd kick on the left ankle, he came galloping round the corner at 40 m.p.h., and even as she braked her car, speculating on his motives in running along the high road at this brisk speed, along came Police Constable Popjoy, doing approximately 55 m.p.h.

When a man doing 55 m.p.h. pursues a man capable of only 40, the end is merely a question of time. On the present occasion it came somewhat sooner than might have been expected owing to Reginald tripping on a loose pebble and falling like a sack of coals. The constable, coming up, bestrode him like a colossus.

'Ho!' he said, for, as has been indicated, he was a man of limited conversational resources, and all the woman in Amanda sprang into sudden life. She would have been the last person to affect to know what all this was about, but it was abundantly plain that the man to whom she had given her heart was in the process of getting pinched by the police and only a helpmeet's gentle hand could save him. Reaching in the tool box, she produced a serviceable spanner and, not letting a twig snap beneath her feet, advanced on the officer from behind. There was a dull, chunky sound as he sank to earth, and Reginald, looking up, saw who it was that had popped up through a trap to his aid. A surge of emotion filled him.

'Oh, hullo,' he said. 'So there you are.'

'That's right.'

'Nice evening.'

'Beautiful. How's everything, Reggie?'

'Smashing, thanks, now that you've socked the flatty.'

'I noticed he was in your hair a bit.'

'He was, rather. You don't think he'll suddenly recover and make a spring, do you?'

'He will be out of circulation for some little time, I imagine. In which respect he differs from me, because I'm back in circulation.'

'Eh?'

'I've broken my engagement to Percy Knubble.'

'Oh, fine.'

'You are the man I love.'

'Oh, finer.'

'And now,' said Amanda, 'let's have the gen. How did you happen to get snarled up with the constabulary?'

She listened with a thoughtful frown as Reginald related the events of the evening. She found herself particularly intrigued by his account of the activities of her Uncle Jasper.

'You say he was sprinkling paraffin hither and thither?'

'Freely.'

'And there were paper and shavings on the floor?'

'In considerable abundance. Rather risky, it seemed to me. You never know when that sort of thing won't start a fire.'

'You're quite right. If he had happened to drop a lighted match.... Look,' said Amanda. 'You go home and de-black yourself. I'll stay here and lend the rozzer a helping hand when he comes to.'

It was some minutes later that Police Constable Popjoy opened his eyes and said: 'Where am I?'

'Right here,' said Amanda. 'Did you see what hit you?'

'No, I didn't.'

'It was that Russian Sputnik thing you've probably read about in the papers.'

'Coo!'

'Coo is correct. They raise a nasty bump, these Sputniks, do they not? That head of yours wants a beefsteak or something slapped on it. Jump into my car and come along with me, and we'll see what the larder of Wissel Hall has to offer.'

Sir Jasper, having used up all the paraffin in the cellar, had left the house to go to the garage for petrol and was approaching the front steps when Amanda drove up. His emotion on beholding her was marked.

'Amanda! I was not expecting you for another two hours.'

The girl alighted from the car and drew him aside.

'So,' she said, 'I rather gathered when Reggie Mulliner told me a few moments ago that he had seen you strewing the floor of the hall with paper and shavings and sprinkling paraffin on them.'

Sir Jasper had not presided over a hundred general meetings for nothing. He preserved his composure. The closest observer, eyeing his face, could not have known that his heart, leaping into his mouth, had just loosened two front teeth. He spoke with the dignified calm which had so often quelled unruly shareholders.

'Absurd! There are no shavings and paper on the floor.'

'Reggie said he saw them.'

'An optical illusion, no doubt.'

'Perhaps you're right. Still, just for fun, I'll go in and look. And I'll take Constable Popjoy with me. I'm sure he will be interested.'

Sir Jasper's heart did another *entrechat*.

'Constable Popjoy?' he quavered.

'He's in my car. I thought it would be a sound move to bring him along.'

Sir Jasper clutched her arm.

'No, do not go in, particularly in the company of P.C. Popjoy. The fact is, my dear, that there is a certain amount of substance in what young Mulliner told you. I did happen to drop a few shavings and a little paper which I was carrying about with me – I cannot remember for what reason – and I carelessly tripped and upset a container of paraffin. It was the sort of thing that might have happened to anyone, but it is possible that a man like Popjoy would draw a wrong conclusion.'

'He might think you were planning to do down the insurance company for a substantial sum.'

'It is conceivable. These policemen are so prone to think the worst.'

'You wouldn't dream of doing a thing like that?'

'Certainly not.'

'Or of sticking poor trusting half-witted baa-lambs with dud

oil stock. Oh, that reminds me, Uncle Jasper. I knew there was
something I wanted to talk to you about. Reggie's changed his
mind about those Smelly River Ordinaries. He doesn't want
them. True,' said Amanda in response to Sir Jasper's remark that
he had jolly well got them. 'But he would like you to buy them
back.'

'He would, would he?'

'I told him you would be delighted.'

'You did, did you?'

'Won't you be delighted?'

'No, I won't.'

'Too bad. Oh, Popjoy.'

'Miss?'

'Kindly step this way.'

'Please!' cried Sir Jasper. 'Please, please, please!'

'One moment, Popjoy. You were saying, Uncle Jasper?'

'If young Mulliner really prefers to sell me back those
shares...'

'He does. This is official. He has taken one of those strange
unaccountable dislikes for them.'

There was silence for a space. Then from Sir Jasper's interior
there proceeded a groan not unlike one of the lower notes of Old
Man River.

'Very well. I agree.'

'Splendid. Popjoy!'

'Miss?'

'Don't step this way.'

'Very good, miss.'

'And now,' said Amanda, 'ho for your study, where I shall
require you to write out a cheque, payable to Reginald Mulliner,
for a hundred thousand pounds.'

Sir Jasper reeled.

'A hundred thousand? He only paid me fifty thousand.'

'The stock has gone up. Surely no one understands better than you these market fluctuations. Close the deal at once, is my advice, before it hits a new high. Or would you prefer that I once more asked Constable Popjoy to navigate in this direction?'

'No, no, no, on no account.'

'Just as you say. Popjoy.'

'Miss?'

'Continue not to step this way.'

'Very good, miss.'

Another groan escaped Sir Jasper. He looked at his niece with infinite reproach.

'So this is how you repay my unremitting kindness! For years I have bestowed on you an uncle's love . . .'

'And now you're going to bestow on Reggie an uncle's hundred thousand pounds.'

A thought struck Sir Jasper.

'I wonder,' he said, 'if instead of a cheque for that sum young Mulliner would not prefer a block of Deep Blue Atlantic stock of equivalent value? It is a company formed for the purpose of extracting gold from sea water, and its possibilities are boundless. I should be surprised – nay, astounded – if anyone investing in it did not secure a return of ninety per centum on his . . .' Sir Jasper broke off as the girl began to speak. 'Yes, yes,' he said, when she had finished. 'Quite, quite. I see what you mean.' He heaved a little sigh. 'It was merely a suggestion.'

As so often happened in August when the citizenry was taking its annual vacation, that popular resort, Bramley-on-Sea, had filled up with ozone-breathers till there was barely standing room. Henry Cuthbert Purkiss, proprietor of the widely read journal for children, *Wee Tots*, was there with Mrs Purkiss. Oofy Prosser, the Drones Club millionaire, was there, staying at the Hôtel Magnifique and looking perfectly foul in a panama hat with a scarlet ribbon. A distinguished visitor from the United States – Wally Judd the cartoonist, the man behind the Dauntless Desmond comic strip which is syndicated in sixteen hundred American papers – was week-ending there. And on the beach in front of the Magnifique an observer, scanning the throng, would have noticed among those present Bingo Little, the able young editor of *Wee Tots*, and his wife Mrs Bingo, better known as the novelist Rosie M. Banks. They were watching their infant son, Algernon Aubrey, build a sand castle.

The day was a bright, beautiful, balmy day, with an anti-cyclone doing its stuff and all nature smiling, but it too frequently occurs in this disturbed postwar world that, when all nature smiles, there are a whole lot of unfortunate toads beneath the harrow who cannot raise so much as a simper, and Bingo was one of them. The sun was shining, but there was no sunshine in his heart. The sky was blue, but he was bluer. It was not the fact that Mrs Bingo was off to London to attend the annual dinner of the Pen and Ink Club that had caused melancholy to mark him for its own, sorely though he always missed her when she went away: what had so lowered his spirits and given the sleeve across the windpipe to his morale was a remark that had just fallen from her lips.

Speaking of the mysterious disappearance of his gold cuff links on the previous day, she was convinced, she said, that a professional cuff-link thief must have been at work, and Bingo was to place the matter immediately in the hands of the police.

'They will go round,' she explained, 'and make enquiries at all the pawn shops.'

It was this that had blotted out the sunshine for Bingo and made him feel, warm though the day was, that centipedes with icy feet were walking up and down his spine. If there was one thing more than another which would be foreign to his policy, it was to have the police making enquiries at these establishments, particularly at the one in Seaview Road. For it was there that yesterday, in order to obtain five pounds with which to back a horse that had come in seventh, he had personally put those cuff links up the spout. And Mrs Bingo's views on that sort of thing were rigid.

'You really think that would be advisable?' he faltered.

'Of course. It's the only thing to do.'

'Throws a lot of extra work on the poor chaps.'

'They are paid for it, and I think they really enjoy the excitement of the chase. Good gracious,' said Mrs Bingo, looking at her watch, 'is that the time? I must be rushing. Goodbye, angel. Take care of Algy.'

'His welfare shall be my constant concern.'

'Don't let him out of your sight for a minute. I'll be back tomorrow night. Goodbye, my precious.'

'Goodbye, tree on which the fruit of my life hangs,' said Bingo, and a moment later was alone with his thoughts.

He was still deep in sombre meditation when a voice at his side said 'Ah, Mr Little. Good morning,' and, emerging from his reverie with a start, he saw that he had with him the Purkisses, Mr and Mrs.

'Kitchy kitchy,' observed the female Purkiss, addressing Algernon Aubrey.

The child treated the remark with silent disdain, and Mrs Purkiss, discouraged, said she must be getting along to keep an appointment with her hairdresser. As she withdrew, a stifled groan burst from Purkiss's lips, and Bingo saw that he was gazing with bulging eyes at the son and heir.

'Ugh!' said Purkiss, shuddering strongly.

'I beg your pardon?' said Bingo. He spoke coldly. He had no illusions about his first-born's appearance, being well aware that though Time, the great healer, would eventually turn Algernon Aubrey into a suave boulevardier like his father, he presented to the eye as of even date, like so many infants of tender years, the aspect of a mass murderer suffering from an ingrowing toenail. Nevertheless he resented this exhibition of naked horror. Purkiss, himself far from being an oil-painting, was, he felt, in no position to criticize.

Purkiss hastened to explain.

'I am sorry,' he said. 'I should not have let my feelings get the better of me. It is just that, situated as I am, the mere sight of the younger generation chills me to the marrow. Mr Little,' said Purkiss, avoiding Algernon Aubrey's eye, for the child was giving him the sort of cold, hard look which Jack Dempsey used to give his opponents in the ring, 'there is to be a Bonny Babies contest here tomorrow, and I have got to act as judge.'

Bingo's hauteur vanished. He could understand the other's emotion, for he knew what an assignment like that involved. Freddie Widgeon of the Drones had once got let in for judging a similar competition in the south of France, and his story of what he had gone through on that occasion had held the club smoking-room spellbound.

'Golly!' he said. 'How did that happen?'

'Mrs Purkiss arranged it. She felt that the appearance of its proprietor in the public eye would stimulate the circulation of *Wee Tots*, bringing in new subscribers. Subscribers!' said Purkiss, waving a passionate hand. 'I don't want subscribers. All I want is to be allowed to enjoy a quiet and peaceful holiday completely free from bonny babies of every description. To be relieved of this hideous burden that has been laid upon me I would give untold gold.'

It was as though an electric shock had passed through Bingo. He leaped perhaps six inches.

'You would?' he said. 'Untold gold?'

'Untold gold.'

'When you say untold gold, would you go as high as a fiver?'

'Certainly, and consider the money well spent.'

'Then hand it over,' said Bingo, 'and in return I will take your place on the judge's rostrum. It will stimulate the circulation of *Wee Tots* just as much if its editor appears in the public eye.'

For an instant ecstasy caused Purkiss to quiver from stem to stern. The word 'Whoopee!' seemed to be trembling on his lips. Then the light died out of his face.

'But what of Mrs Purkiss? She has issued her orders. How can I disobey them?'

'My dear Purkiss, use the loaf. All you have to do is sprain your ankle or dislocate your spine or something. Fall out of a window. Get run over by a lorry. Any lorry driver will be glad to run over you, if you slip him a couple of bob. Then you will be set. Obviously the old geezer ... I should say Mrs Purkiss ... can't expect you to go bounding about judging bonny babies if you are lying crippled on a chesterfield of pain. You were saying something about a fiver, Purkiss. I should be glad to see the colour of your money.'

As in a dream, Purkiss produced a five-pound note. As in a dream, he handed it over. As in a dream, Bingo took it.

'Mr Little—' Purkiss began. Then words failed him, and with a defiant look at Algernon Aubrey such as an Indian coolie, safe up a tree, might have given the baffled crocodile at the foot of it, he strode away humming a gay air, his hat on the side of his head. And Bingo was gazing lovingly at the bank note and on the point of giving it a hearty kiss, when a nippy little breeze, springing up from the sea, blew it out of his hand and it went fluttering away in the direction of the esplanade as if equipped with wings.

It was a situation well calculated to nonplus the keenest-witted. It nonplussed Bingo completely. His primary impulse, of course, was to follow his lost treasure as it flew, it taking the high road and himself the low road, but even as he braced his muscles for the quick cross-country run there flashed into his mind those parting words of Mrs Bingo's about not letting Algernon Aubrey out of his sight. He knew what had been the thought behind them. Let out of sight, the child might well wander into the sea and go down for the third time or get on the wrong side of the law by hitting some holiday-maker on the head with his spade. None knew better than he how prone the little fellow was to cleave the casques of men, as the poet said, if you put a spade in his hands. There was a certain type of Homburg hat which had always proved irresistible to him.

It was borne in upon Bingo that he was on what is generally called the horns of a dilemma. He stood there, like Hamlet, moody and irresolute, and while he hesitated the issue was taken out of his hands. The five-pound note fluttered down into a car which was on the point of starting, and its driver, gathering it up with a look on his face that suggested a sudden conviction that the age of miracles was still with us, drove off.

It was some ten minutes later that Bingo, who had spent most of those ten minutes with his head buried in his hands, tottered on to the esplanade with Algernon Aubrey in his arms and was passing the door of the Hôtel Magnifique, when Oofy Prosser came out.

The poet Wordsworth has told us that his heart was accustomed to leap up when he beheld a rainbow in the sky, and this was how Bingo's heart behaved when he beheld Oofy Prosser. It was not that Oofy was a thing of beauty ... his pimples alone would have kept him out of the rainbow class ... but he had that quality which so many disgustingly rich men have of looking disgustingly rich. And in addition to being disgustingly rich, he was Algernon Aubrey's godfather. It was with hope dawning in his soul that Bingo bounded forward.

'Oofy, old man!'

Observing what it was that Bingo was carrying, Oofy backed hastily.

'Hey!' he exclaimed. 'Don't point that thing at me!'

'It's only my baby.'

'I dare say. But point it the other way.'

'I think he wants to kiss you.'

'Stand back!' cried Oofy, brandishing his panama hat. 'I am armed!'

It seemed to Bingo that the conversation was straying from the right lines. He hastened to change the subject.

'I wonder if you have noticed, Oofy, that I am pale and haggard?' he said.

'You look all right to me. At least,' said Oofy, qualifying this statement, 'as right as you ever do.'

'Ah, then, it doesn't show. I'm surprised. I should have thought it would have done. For I am in desperate straits, Oofy. If I don't get hold of someone who will lend me a fiver—'

'Very hard to find, that type of man. Why do you want a fiver?'

Bingo was only too ready to explain. He knew Oofy Prosser to be a man allergic to sharing the wealth, but his, he felt, was a story calculated to break down the toughest sales resistance. In accents broken with emotion he told it from its earliest beginnings to this final ghastly tragedy that had befallen him. When he had finished, Oofy remained for some moments plunged in thought. Then his eyes, generally rather dull, lit up, as if the thought into which he had been plunged had produced an inspiration.

'You say you're judging this Bonny Babies thing?'

'Yes, but that doesn't get me anywhere. I can't ask Purkiss for another fiver.'

'You don't have to. As I see it, the matter is quite simple. Your primary object is to divert your wife's mind from gold cuff links and pawn shops – to give her, in other words, something else to think about. Very well. Enter that little gargoyle of yours and award him the first prize, and she will be so delighted that gold cuff links will fade out of her mind. I guarantee this. I am not a mother myself, but I understand a mother's heart from soup to nuts. In her pride at the young plugugly's triumph everything else will be forgotten.'

Bingo stared. It seemed to him that the other's brain, that brain whose subtle scheming had so often chiselled fellow members of the Drones out of half-crowns and even larger sums, must have blown a fuse.

'But, Oofy, old man, reflect. If I judge a Bonny Babies contest and raise the hand of my personal baby with the words "The winnah!", I shall be roughly handled, if not lynched. These mothers are tough stuff. You were there when Freddie Widgeon was telling us about what happened to him at Cannes.'

Oofy clicked his tongue impatiently.

'Naturally I had not overlooked an obvious point like that. The child will not be entered as whatever-its-ghastly-name-is Little, but as whatever-its-ghastly-name-is Prosser. Putting it in words of one syllable, I will bring the young thug to the trysting place, affecting to be its uncle. You will then, after careful consideration, award it the first prize. And if you're worrying about whether such a scheme is strictly honest, forget it. The prize will only be an all-day sucker or a woolly muffler or something. It isn't as if money were involved.'

'Something in that.'

'There is everything in that. If money entered into it, I would never dream of suggesting such a ruse,' said Oofy virtuously. 'But who cares who wins a woolly muffler? Well, there it is. Take it or leave it. I'm simply trying to do the friendly thing and keep your home from being in the melting pot. I take it I am right in assuming that if this business of the cuff links comes out, your home will be in the melting pot?'

'Yes, right in the melting pot.'

'Then I would certainly advise you to adopt my plan. You will?

Fine. Excuse me a moment,' said Oofy. 'I have to make a telephone call.'

He went into the hotel, rang up his bookmaker in London,
and the following conversation ensued.

'Mr McAlpin?'

'Speaking.'

'This is Mr Prosser.'

'Oh, yes?'

'Listen, Mr McAlpin, I'm down at Bramley-on-Sea, and they
are having a Bonny Babies contest tomorrow. I'm entering my
little nephew.'

'Oh, yes?'

'And I thought it would add to the interest of the proceedings if I had a small bet on. Do your activities as a turf
accountant extend to accepting wagers on seaside Bonny Baby
competitions?'

'Certainly. We cover all sporting events.'

'What odds will you give against the Prosser colt?'

'Your nephew, you say?'

'That's right.'

'Does he look like you?'

'There is quite a resemblance.'

'Then you can have fifty to one.'

'Right. In tenners.'

Oofy returned to Bingo.

'The only thing I'm afraid of,' he said, 'is that when it comes
to the acid test, you may lose your nerve.'

'Oh, I won't.'

'You might, if there were no added inducement. So I'll tell you
what I'll do. The moment you have given your decision, I will
slip you five pounds and you will be able to take the cuff links out

of pawn, thus avoiding all unpleasantness in the unlikely event of your wife continuing to bear them in mind despite her child's triumph. May as well be on the safe side.'

Bingo could not speak. His heart was too full for words. The only thing that kept his happiness from being perfect was a sudden fear lest, before the event could take place, Oofy might be snatched up to heaven in a fiery chariot.

Nevertheless, as he made his way to the arena on the following afternoon, he was conscious of distinct qualms and flutterings. And his apprehensions were not relieved by the sight of the assembled competitors.

True, the great majority of the entrants had that indefinable something in their appearance that suggested that if the police were not spreading dragnets for them, they were being very negligent in their duties, but fully a dozen were so comparatively human that he could see that it was going to cause comment when he passed them over in favour of Algernon Aubrey. Questions would be asked, investigations made. Quite possibly he would be had up before the Jockey Club and warned off the turf.

However, with the vast issues at stake there was nothing to do but stiffen the sinews, summon up the blood and have a go at it, so proceeding to the platform he bowed to the applause of what looked to him like about three hundred and forty-seven mothers, all ferocious, raised a hand to check – if possible – the howling of their offspring, and embarked on the speech which he had been at pains to prepare in the watches of the night.

He spoke of England's future, which, he pointed out, must rest on these babies and others like them, adding that he scarcely need remind them that the England to which he alluded had been described by the poet Shakespeare as this royal throne of kings, this sceptred isle, this earth of majesty, this seat of Mars, this other Eden, demi-Paradise, this fortress built by nature for herself against infection and the hand of war. Than which, he thought they would all agree with him, nothing could be fairer.

He spoke of *Wee Tots*, putting in a powerful build-up for the dear old sheet and urging one and all to take advantage of the easy subscription terms now in operation.

He spoke – and here his manner took on a new earnestness – of the good, clean spirit of fair play which has made England what it is – the spirit which, he was confident, would lead all the mothers present to accept the judge's decision, even should it go against their own nominees, with that quiet British sportsmanship which other nations envy so much. He had a friend, he said, who, acting as judge of a Baby Contest in the south of France, had been chased for a quarter of a mile along the waterfront by indignant mothers of Hon. Mentions armed with knives and hat pins. That sort of thing could never happen at Bramley-on-Sea. No, no. English mothers were not like that. And while on this subject, he said, striking a lighter note, he was reminded of a little story of two Irishmen who were walking up Broadway, which may be new to some of you present here this afternoon.

The story went well. A studio television audience could hardly have laughed more heartily. But though he acknowledged the guffaws with a bright smile, inwardly his soul had begun to shrink like a salted snail. Time was passing, and there were no signs of Oofy and his precious burden. Long 'ere this he should have rolled up with the makings.

He resumed his speech. He told another story about two Scotsmen who were walking down Sauchiehall Street in Glasgow. But now his comedy had lost its magic and failed to grip. A peevish voice said 'Get on with it', and the sentiment plainly pleased the gathering. As he began a third story about two Cockneys who were standing on a street corner in Whitechapel, possibly a hundred peevish voices said 'Get on with it', and shortly after that perhaps a hundred and fifty.

And still no Oofy.

Five minutes later, the popular clamour for a showdown having taken on a resemblance to the howling of timber wolves in a Canadian forest, he was compelled to act. With ashen face he awarded the handsome knitted woolly jacket to a child selected at random from the sea of faces beneath him and sank into a chair, a broken man.

And as he sat there, trying not to let his mind dwell on the shape of things to come, a finger tapped him on the shoulder and he looked up and saw standing beside him a policeman.

'Mr Little?' said the policeman.

Bingo, still dazed, said Yes, he thought so.

'I shall have to ask you to come along with me,' said the policeman.

Other policemen on other occasions, notably on the night of the annual aquatic encounter on the River Thames between the rival crews of the Universities of Oxford and Cambridge, had made the same observation to Bingo, and on such occasions he had always found it best to go quietly. He rose and accompanied the officer to the door, and with a curiosity perhaps natural in the circumstances asked why he was being pinched.

'Not pinched, sir,' said the policeman, as they walked off. 'You're wanted at the station to identify an accused ... if you *can* identify him. His statement is that he's a friend of yours and was acting with your cognisance and approval.'

'I don't follow you, officer,' said Bingo, who did not follow the officer. 'Acting how?'

'Taking your baby for an airing, sir. He claims that you instructed him to do so. It transpired this way. Accused was observed by a Mrs Purkiss with your baby on his person slinking along the public thoroughfare. He was a man of furtive aspect in a panama hat with a scarlet ribbon, and Mrs Purkiss, recognizing the baby, said to herself "Cor lumme, stone the crows!".'

'She said . . . what was that line of Mrs Purkiss's again?'

'"Cor lumme, stone the crows!" sir. The lady's suspicions having been aroused, she summoned a constable and gave accused in charge as a kidnapper, and after a certain amount of fuss and unpleasantness he was conducted to the station and deposited in a cell. Prosser he said his name was. Is the name Prosser familiar to you, sir?'

The Officer's statement that there had been a certain amount of fuss and unpleasantness involved in the process of getting the accused Prosser to the police station was borne out by the latter's appearance when he was led into Bingo's presence. He had a black eye and his collar had been torn from the parent stud. The other eye, the one that was still open, gleamed with fury and what was patently a loathing for the human species.

The sergeant who was seated at the desk invited Bingo to inspect the exhibit.

'This man says he knows you.'

'That's right.'

'Friend of yours?'

'Bosom.'

'And you gave him your baby?'

'Well, you could put it that way. More on loan, of course.'

'Ho!' said the sergeant, speaking like a tiger of the jungle deprived of its prey, if tigers of the jungle in those circumstances do say 'Ho'! 'You're quite sure?'

'Oh, rather.'

'So sucks to you, sergeant!' said Oofy. 'And now,' he went on haughtily, 'I presume that I am at liberty to go.'

'You do, do you? Then you pre-blinking-well-sume wrong,' said the sergeant, brightening at the thought that he was at least going to save something from the wreck of his hopes and dreams. 'Not by any manner of means you aren't at liberty to go. There's this matter of obstructing the police in the execution of their duty. You punched Constable Wilks in the abdomen.'

'And I'd do it again.'

'Not for a fortnight or fourteen days you won't,' said the sergeant, now quite his cheerful self once more. 'The Bench is going to take a serious view of that, a very serious view. All right, constable, remove the prisoner.'

'Just a second,' said Bingo, though something seemed to tell him that this was not quite the moment. 'Could I have that fiver, Oofy?'

His suspicions were proved correct. It was not the moment. Oofy did not reply. He gave Bingo a long, lingering look from the eye which was still functioning, and the arm of the law led him out. And Bingo had started to totter off, when the sergeant reminded him that there was something he was forgetting.

'Your baby, sir.'

'Oh, ah, yes.'

'Shall we send it, or do you want to take it with you?'

'Oh, with me. Yes, certainly with me.'

'Very good,' said the sergeant. 'I'll have it wrapped up.'

Referring back to the beginning of this chronicle, we see that we compared Bingo Little, when conversing with his wife Rosie on the subject of police and pawn shops, to a toad beneath the harrow. As he sat with Algernon Aubrey on the beach some quarter of an hour after parting from the sergeant, the illusion that he was what Webster's Dictionary describes as a terrestrial member of the frog family and that somebody was driving spikes through his sensitive soul had become intensified. He viewed the future with concern, and would greatly have preferred not to be compelled to view it at all. Already he could hear the sharp intake of the wifely breath and the spate of wifely words which must inevitably follow the stammering confession of his guilt. He and Rosie had always been like a couple of turtle-doves, but he knew only too well that when the conditions are right, a female turtle-dove can express herself with a vigour which a Caribbean hurricane might envy.

Emerging with a shudder from this unpleasant reverie, he found that Algernon Aubrey had strayed from his side and, looking to the south-east, observed him some little distance away along the beach. The child was hitting a man in a Homburg hat over the head with his spade, using, it seemed to Bingo, a good deal of wristy follow-through. (In hitting men in Homburg hats over the head with spades, the follow-through is everything.)

He rose, and hurried across to where the party of the second part sat rubbing his occipital bone. In his capacity of Algernon Aubrey's social sponsor he felt that an apology was due from him.

'I say,' he said, 'I'm most frightfully sorry about my baby socking you like that. Wouldn't have had it happen for the world. But I'm afraid he never can resist a Homburg hat. They seem to draw him like a magnet.'

The man, who was long and thin and horn-rimmed-spectacled, did not reply for a moment. He was staring at Algernon Aubrey like one who sees visions.

'Is this your baby?' he said.

Bingo said Yes, sir, that was his baby, and the man muttered something about this being his lucky day.

'What a find!' he said. 'Talk about manna from heaven! I'd like to draw him, if I may. We must put the thing on a business basis, of course. I take it that you are empowered to act as his agent. Shall we say five pounds?'

Bingo shook his head sadly.

'I'm afraid it's off,' he said. 'I haven't any money. I can't pay you.'

'You don't pay me. I pay you,' said the man. 'So if five pounds is all right with you . . .' He broke off, directed another searching glance at Algernon Aubrey and seemed to change his mind. 'No, not five. It would be a steal. Let's make it ten.'

Bingo gasped. Bramley-on-Sea was flickering before his eyes like a Western on the television screen. For an instant the thought crossed his mind that this must be his guardian angel buckling down to work after a prolonged period of loafing on his job. Then, his vision clearing, he saw that the other had no wings. He had spoken, moreover, with an American intonation, and the guardian angel of a member of the Drones Club would have had an Oxford accent.

'Ten pounds?' he gurgled. 'Did I understand you to say that you would give me ten pounds?'

'I meant twenty, and it's worth every cent of the money. Here you are,' said the man, producing notes from an inside pocket.

Bingo took them reverently and, taught by experience, held on to them like a barnacle attaching itself to the hull of a ship.

'When would you like to start painting Algy's portrait?'

The man's horn-rimmed spectacles flashed fire.

'Good God!' he cried, revolted. 'You don't think I'm a portrait painter, do you? I'm Wally Judd.'

'Wally who?'

'Judd. The Dauntless Desmond man.'

'The what man?'

'Don't you know Dauntless Desmond?'

'I'm afraid I don't.'

The other drew a deep breath.

'I never thought to hear those words in a civilized country. Dauntless Desmond, my comic strip. It's running in the *Mirror* and in sixteen hundred papers in America. Dauntless Desmond, the crooks' despair.'

'He is a detective, this D. Desmond?'

'A private eye or shamus,' corrected the other. 'And he's always up against the creatures of the underworld. He's as brave as a lion.'

'Sounds like a nice chap.'

'He is. One of the best. But there's a snag. Desmond is impulsive. He will go bumping off these creatures of the underworld. He shoots them in the stomach. Well, I needn't tell you what that sort of thing leads to.'

'The supply of creatures of the underworld is beginning to give out?'

'Exactly. There is a constant need for fresh faces, and the moment I saw your baby I knew I had found one. That lowering look! Those hard eyes which could be grafted on the head of a man-eating shark and no questions asked. He's a natural. Could you bring him around to the Hôtel Splendide right away, so that I can do some preliminary sketches?'

A sigh of ecstasy escaped Bingo. It set the bank notes in his pocket crackling musically, and for a moment he stood there listening as to the strains of some great anthem.

'Make it half an hour from now,' he said. 'I have to look in first on a fellow I know in Seaview Road.'

When Walter Judson got engaged to Angela Pirbright, who had been spending the summer in our little community as the guest of her aunt, Mrs Lavender Botts, we were all very pleased about it. The ideal match, everybody considered, and I agreed with them. As the golf club's Oldest Member, I had been watching young couples pairing off almost back to the days of the gutty ball, but few so admirably suited to each other as these twain, he so stalwart and virile, she a girl whose outer crust bore a strong resemblance to that of Miss Marilyn Monroe. It was true that he played golf and she tennis, but these little differences can always be adjusted after marriage. There seemed no cloud on the horizon.

I was surprised, accordingly, when Walter came to me one afternoon as I sat in my chair on the terrace overlooking the ninth green, to note on his face a drawn, haggard look, the sort of look a man wears when one of his drives, intended to go due north, has gone nor'nor'-east. Of that sunny smile of his, which had been the talk of the place for weeks, there was no sign.

'Something the matter, my boy?' I asked, concerned.

'Only doom, disaster, desolation and despair,' he said, scowling darkly at a fly which had joined us and was doing callisthenics on the rim of my glass. 'You have probably heard that tomorrow I play George Porter in the final of the President's Cup.'

'I am refereeing the match.'

'Oh, are you? Then you will have a front row seat at the tragedy and will get a good view when my life is blighted and the cup of happiness dashed from my lips.'

I frowned. I did not approve of this sort of talk from a young man in the springtime of life. I would not have liked it much even from someone more elderly.

'Come, come,' I said. 'Don't falter, Walter. Why this defeatist attitude? From what people tell me, George Porter will be less than the dust beneath your chariot wheels. I think you will beat him.'

'I don't, and I'll tell you why. You know the Botts family?'

I did indeed, and spent a considerable portion of my time avoiding them. The head of the house, Mrs Lavender Botts, had a distressing habit of writing books and talking a good deal about them. Her works were not novels. I am a broadminded man and can tolerate female novelists, but Mrs Botts gave English litera-ture a bad name by turning out those unpleasant whimsical things to which women of her type are so addicted. *My Chums The Pixies* was one of her titles, *How To Talk To The Flowers* another, and *Many Of My Best Friends Are Field Mice* a third. The rumour had got about that she was contemplating a fourth volume on the subject of elves.

Ponsford Botts, her husband, told dialect stories, and perhaps even harder to bear was their elder son, Cosmo, a Civil Servant by profession who reviewed books for various weekly papers and like so many book reviewers had a distressing tendency to set everybody right about everything. Strong men had often hidden behind trees when they saw Cosmo coming.

'Yes, I am fairly Botts-conscious,' I said. 'Why do you ask?'

His voice shook a little as he replied.

'I have just heard they are going to walk round with me tomorrow.'

I saw what he had in mind.

'You think they will put you off your game?'

'I know they will, but that's not the worst. Angela will be there, too. You see the frightful peril that looms?'

I said no, I didn't, and he muttered something about somebody, whose name I did not catch, being a fatheaded ivory-skulled old dumb-bell.

'Surely it's obvious? You've seen me play golf, haven't you?'

'Oddly enough, no, except when driving off the first tee or holing out at the ninth. No doubt I missed a genuine treat, but I find it pleasanter these days to remain in my chair on this terrace. Why?'

'Because, if you had, you would know that once on the course I become a changed man. In ordinary life calm, suave and courtly, the moment I am out on the links and things go wrong, as they always do, the fiend that sleeps in me is awakened. I curse my caddy, I snarl at spectators, I make a regular exhibition of myself. And tomorrow, as I say, the air will be thick with Bottses, each rasping my nervous system in his or her individual way. And Angela will be there, looking on.'

I nodded gravely.

'You think that something will pop?'

'I don't see how it can be avoided. Picture what will happen if just as I have missed a short putt old Botts starts telling me the story of the two costermongers who went to heaven, or Ma Botts brings up the subject of elves, or Cosmo explains how he would have made the shot. Yes, unquestionably something will pop.'

'And you fear the effect this generous wrath of yours will have on your betrothed?'

'Well, figure it out for yourself. She thinks she is linking her lot with a Chevalier Bayard. What will be her reaction when she finds that what she has really drawn is a Captain Bligh of the *Bounty*? I'll tell you what her reaction will be. She will recoil from me in horror and cancel all orders for the trousseau before I can say "Henry Cotton". And quite understandably. I wouldn't want to marry Captain Bligh of the *Bounty* myself.'

'But I thought the angry young man was all the go nowadays.'

'Not if he is as angry as I get when I miss a short putt. And the shock will be all the greater because up till now I have always gone out of my way to be deferential and courteous to these human streptococci. The strain was fearful, but for Angela's sake I stifled my true opinion of them and wore the mask. The urge to tell them to go and boil their respective heads was very strong, but I resisted it.'

'You feel that she would have taken in bad part the suggestion that they should go and boil their heads?'

'Of course she would. She has a niece's love for Ma Botts, the same for Pa Botts, and a cousin's love – though I don't see how she manages it – for Cosmo Botts, and had I revealed what I really thought of them, would have been as sore as a gumboil and might even have given me the bum's rush. As it is, I am not sure that I may not have given her some inkling of the truth, for her manner has been strange of late. I catch her looking at me in a speculating sort of way, as if she suspected.'

'Imagination.'

'It may be so, but it doesn't matter one way or the other, for tomorrow she will know all. So now you see what I had in mind when I spoke just now of doom, disaster, desolation and despair.'

His problem was one that undoubtedly presented many points of interest, and fortunately I was in a position to solve it.

'What you need,' I said, 'is self-control, and I will tell you how you can achieve it. In my playing days I, like you, was inclined to become a little emotional on the golf course. I cured myself by thinking of Socrates.'

'The Greek bozo?'

'The, as you say, Greek bozo. Job would probably have answered equally well, but for some reason I preferred Socrates.'

'I don't seem to follow you. How does Socrates get into the act?'

'Perfectly simple. He, if you remember, had his troubles ... it can't have been at all pleasant for him to have to drink that bowl of hemlock ... but he refused to let them get him down, bearing them consistently with good-humoured calm and a stiff upper lip. So if you keep reminding yourself that even if your best shots end up in bunkers you are much better off than he was, and murmur "Socrates" to yourself at intervals – or, better, "Socks" ... no, I have it. I shall be with you tomorrow, and every time I notice that you are about to erupt I will whisper the magic word in your ear. That ought to do the trick.'

'It solves the whole thing. I see myself getting through the final of the President's Cup without a stain on my character. What was it you were saying – that people were saying that George Porter would be beneath my chariot wheels?'

'Less than the dust.'

'They said a mouthful,' said Walter, now completely restored to his customary equanimity, and with a gay 'Socks' on his lips went off to the bar for a gin and tonic.

He was on the first tee with Angela when I arrived there on the following afternoon, chatting chummily of this and that. Nobody else was present. The annual contest for the President's

Cup never draws the dense crowd of spectators which you see at some such event as the British Open. Its high-sounding title is perhaps a little misleading, for it is not one of our big competitions. Entries are accepted only from those whose handicap is not lower than eighteen, it having been designed as a special treat for the underprivileged submerged tenth of our golfing world. It brings out the rabbits as if it were a conjuror extracting them from a silk hat.

George Porter and Walter both had handicaps of eighteen, but I had been told by those who had watched them that there was a marked difference between them in action. George, these eye-witnesses said, played a steady game. He was a vegetarian and teetotaller, and teetotal vegetarians all play a steady game, due, I think, to the essential vitamins in the grated carrots. Walter, on the other hand, was one of those uncertain performers, varying between a dashing scratch and a shaky thirty-six. Which W. Judson, I was asking myself, should we see this afternoon – the masterful stylist who had once done the long seventh in three or his alter ego who frequently took a spotty eleven at the short second?

It was good, at any rate, whatever the future might bring, to note that at the moment he was still plainly in the best of spirits, these appearing to be not in the least damped by the advent at this point of Mr and Mrs Botts. They were not accompanied by their son Cosmo, he, they said, having been detained at home by a rush order from the *Booksy Weekly* for an article on Albert Camus And The Aesthetic Tradition. They held out hopes that he would be joining us at the turn, and Walter said 'Capital, capital, capital.' A few moments later he drew me aside and revealed the reason for his exuberance. George Porter, it seemed, was in the poorest shape owing to an overnight rift with his fiancée. The local grapevine reported that relations between the two had been severed. From a reliable source Walter had learned that his rival had spent the morning in the bar, sullenly drinking glass after glass of barley-water, and the view he took was that the President's Cup was as good as on his mantelpiece.

'If I can't extract the stuffing from a fellow who has received the ring and letters back and is full to the brim with barley-water,' he said jubilantly, 'I'll never show myself on a golf course again. See, here he comes, looking licked to a splinter.'

It was true. George Porter, who had just appeared, gave the impression, as he advanced towards us on leaden feet, of having had his insides removed by a taxidermist who had absent-mindedly forgotten to complete the operation by stuffing him. I believe this often happens when a young lover has been handed his hat by the adored object. He groaned civilly in response to my greeting, and in a hollow voice called Tails – correctly – when Walter spun the coin for the honour. With bowed head he took his place on the first tee, and the match began.

It speedily became evident that Walter, in predicting a one-sided contest, had not erred. What ensued was a mere massacre, and I am not ashamed to say that, pro-Walter though I was, my heart bled for George Porter. It was plain that the unfortunate man felt his position deeply. It is bad enough to lose the girl you love after spending a fortune on her for months in the matter of flowers and chocolates, and when in addition to this the pants are being trimmed off you in an important golf match the nadir of depression is reached. I have said that George Porter's head was bowed, but his trouble was that he did not keep it bowed. Too often, when making a shot, he would raise it heavenwards, as if asking why a good man should be persecuted like this, which of course resulted in topping. And in sharp contradistinction to his pitiful efforts Walter, striking an inspired vein, was playing superbly.

Golf in its essence is a simple game. All you have to do is hit the ball hard in the right direction. Walter, if he hit the ball at all, always hit it hard, and by the law of averages there was bound to come a day sooner or later when he hit it in the right direction. It had come this afternoon, and I was not surprised that he found himself three up at the turn. His lead would have been even more substantial, had he not at two of the short holes overdriven the green by some fifty yards, while on the ninth the same excess of zeal caused him to miss the cup four times in succession.

There was a brief intermission here while Walter genially permitted his opponent a breathing spell in which he could regroup his shattered forces. George Porter wandered off a little way, to be alone with his grief, and Walter held a sort of court on the tenth tee.

The suavity of his manner had never been more pronounced. He was all courteous attention when Mrs Botts brought the conversation round to elves. Those little beetles you saw crawling on the turf were really elves, she said, and when she mentioned that she was thinking of calling her forthcoming book *Elves On The Golf Course* nothing could have exceeded the warm enthusiasm with which Walter agreed that that was the stuff to give them. Ponsford Botts once more told his story of the two costermongers who went to heaven, and even though he told it with a Swedish dialect Walter laughed unstintedly. He also patted his caddy on the head, and when Cosmo Botts appeared from the clubhouse greeted him like a brother. It seemed to me that in appointing myself his guardian angel this afternoon I had taken on a sinecure.

I mentioned this to Walter when I managed to get him alone for an instant, and he agreed with me.

'It was a good idea,' he said, 'but, as things have turned out, quite unnecessary. Why should I bother to start thinking of Socrates when I am enjoying a pleasant round of golf, right at the peak of my form and with my loved ones about me?'

'Would you call them loved ones?'

'Technically, being relatives of Angela's, they are loved ones. A charming family, in my opinion.'

'Mrs Botts?'

'Delightful woman. Most informative about elves.'

'Mr Botts?'

'Very droll and entertaining. Hard to keep a straight face when he tells those stories of his.'

'Cosmo Botts?'

Here he hesitated for a moment, but speedily rallied.

'A most interesting, cultured young man. Knows a lot. He was telling me just now that he would give me a tip or two for improving my game on the next Nine. Very civil of him, I thought it.'

I was rejoiced to find his morale so high and had started to say so, when my eye was caught by something that was happening on the George Porter sector. A girl was tripping across the greensward towards him, a girl with chestnut hair and a turned-up nose, in whom I recognized Mabel Case, his ex-fiancée. But there was nothing ex about her behaviour now. Scarcely had my gaze rested upon her, when she flung herself on George's neck and kissed him fondly. Apparently something in the nature of a lovers' reconciliation was taking place, and George, as he bade her a tender farewell and came striding buoyantly to the tee, was plainly a new man. His eye was bright, his walk lissom, and he swung his driver like whoever it was who used to swing the sword Excalibur.

'Gosh!' he cried. 'I feel as if a rich uncle in Australia had just handed in his dinner pail and left me a million sterling. What a beautiful world this is! And what a lovely day! The air's like orange juice. How do we stand? Three down, am I not? Well, well, we will soon adjust that state of affairs.'

And waggling gaily he sent a snorter screaming down the fairway, to come to rest within comfortable distance of the green.

'Ha!' he said with satisfaction. 'I don't want that one back and, for your information, there are lots more where that came from.'

I could see that Walter was shaken. He had not budgeted for this sensationally abrupt switch in the orderly run of things. To him, I should imagine, it was as though George Porter had risen from the tomb. His lower jaw, as he teed up his ball, was drooping quite perceptibly. He drove weakly, and his ball fell into the rough.

'My dear fellow, oh my dear fellow!' said Cosmo Botts. 'Let me tell you where you went wrong there. You made the mistake so many high handicap men make, of neglecting to pivot properly. Your hips were locked, and as a result the entire body was tense and awkward. When a full back swing is taken under such conditions, the head will necessarily be pulled away from the fixed position in which it should remain throughout the swing.'

I heard Walter draw a deep breath.

'Or do you think *Elves In The Sunshine* would be a better title?' said Mrs Botts.

An ominous quiver ran through Walter's frame, and I hastened to administer first aid.

'Socks, Walter!'

He stood for an instant rigid. Then he relaxed.

'Socks it is,' he whispered.

'The position as I see it,' said George Porter some minutes later, 'is that I am two down...'

'Now one down,' he added, a few minutes after that.

'And now,' he said, another interval having elapsed, 'all square. Tough luck on you, foozling that chip shot.'

The chip shot to which he referred had been a simple one of about twenty feet from a good lie, and Walter would undoubtedly have made it successfully, had not a sudden strangled sound proceeding from his caddy caused him to jump convulsively and top. He now turned to the child, swelling like a balloon, and once more I sprang into the breach.

'Socks, Walter!'

There was fine stuff in Walter Judson. With an effort painful to watch he controlled himself.

'My dear little fellow,' he said gently, 'you will not be offended if I ask you to try not to make those funny noises while I am playing a shot? They disturb concentration.'

The lad explained that he had got the hiccups, and Walter nodded understandingly.

'Too bad,' he said. 'I think, if I were you, I would trot off and consult my medical adviser. These things are serious, if neglected. I can carry my bag for the rest of the way.'

As the stripling withdrew, I observed Ponsford Botts shaking like a jelly, his invariable habit when a story was coming to the surface.

'Talking of hiccups,' he said, 'have you heard the one about the two Scotsmen?'

Cosmo pursed his lips.

'Are you going to do Scottish dialect?'

'Certainly.'

'I wouldn't.'

'Why not?'

'Apt to make the nose bleed.'

'Nonsense,' said Ponsford Botts, and began. But Cosmo was right. No man can tell with impunity a story involving both Scottish dialect and hiccups. The end is inevitable. Scarcely had he reached the second 'Och, mon' when he was obliged to hurry off to the clubhouse, accompanied by what Walter would have called his loved ones, a handkerchief to his face. As Cosmo's 'I told you so' died away in the distance, I saw a strange new light come into Walter's eyes. It needed no words to tell me what was in his mind. Now, he was saying to himself, he would be able to glue his attention to the game with no distractions in the way of pixies, elves, Scotsmen, hiccups and criticism of his method of playing his shots. All square, with six holes to go and only a vegetarian teetotaller to beat . . . I could see that he was regarding victory as within his grasp.

And such was the fury of his whirlwind onslaught that he won the thirteenth and fourteenth with ease. But then he struck one of those bad patches which come to all golfers, taking an eight on the fifteenth and on the sixteenth a nine. And as George Porter, with his steady game, took sevens, they came to the seventeenth all square once more. Here, recovering, Walter contrived to halve, and everything rested now on what fate held in store for the final spasm.

The eighteenth was a short hole, and even the sort of golfers who played for the President's Cup seldom found any difficulty in reaching the green with their second. Both men were on with nice twos, but whereas George was a dozen feet away, some Act of God had deposited Walter's ball a mere matter of inches from the cup.

'And now,' said Walter, when George Porter, valiant to the last, had laid a steady approach putt dead, 'the mere formality of stuffing it in.'

There are several putting methods in vogue among the lower classes of golf – to name but three, the Sitting Hen, the Paralytic Crouch and the Lumbago Stoop. Walter favoured the Sitting Hen. And he had lowered himself into position and was addressing his ball, when Cosmo Botts, who with Mrs Botts and Angela had returned from ministering to Ponsford Botts, said 'One moment, my dear fellow.'

Walter straightened himself, and gave him a hard look.

'Yes?'

'No, never mind,' said Cosmo. 'I was forgetting that spectators must not give advice to players. Criticism after the shot, yes, advice before it, no. I was only going to tell you that you were doing it all wrong. Carry on, my dear fellow, carry on.'

Walter gave him another hard look, and lowered himself again. And just as he brought the clubhead down, Mrs Botts uttered a piercing shriek.

'Oh, I'm so sorry,' she said, as the ball, struck with a violence which would have been more suitable to the tee than to the putting green, disappeared into a distant bunker. 'I didn't want to disturb you, but there was a dear little beetle just in front of your ball, and I was so afraid you would give it a nasty bang.'

Rising from the Sitting Hen position is as a rule a slow process, reminiscent of a contortionist unscrambling himself after a difficult trick, but Walter seemed to accomplish it in a flash. One moment, he was tied in an apparently inextricable knot, the next, drawn to his full height, his face crimson, his eyes rolling, the sound of his breathing like that of two Scotsmen having hiccups in a Ponsford Botts story. One glance was sufficient to tell me that now was the time for all good men to come to the aid of the party.

'Socks, Walter!' I cried hastily.

'Socks be blowed!' he retorted, and brushing me aside began to speak.

His voice was clear and audible, and I heard Angela give a sharp gasp. And unquestionably what he was saying was of a nature to make any girl gasp sharply.

It was a sort of general critique, expressed with fearless frankness, of Mrs Lavender Botts's manners, morals, intelligence and appearance, together with those of her son Cosmo Botts. And saddened though I was that at the eleventh hour this disaster should have occurred, I could not but admire his choice of words. Long before he had reached his peroration, Mrs Botts, Cosmo at her side, was racing for the clubhouse with ashen face.

Deprived of their society, Walter filled in with a little soliloquizing. And then suddenly it was as if he had awakened from a trance. His shoulders sagged. The putter slipped from his grasp.

He had seen Angela.

'Oh, hullo,' he said dully. 'You back?'

'I have been here some time,' said Angela.

He nodded sombrely.

'Were you listening, by any chance?'

'I was.'

'Then you realize now the sort of man I am. A . . . what's the expression?'

'Fiend in human shape?'

'That's right. Fiend in human shape.'

'Just the kind of fiend I like,' said Angela.

He stared incredulously.

'You mean you don't recoil from me in horror?'

'Not by a jugful,' said the girl, and even from where I stood I could see the lovelight in her eyes. 'I admire you intensely. It was about time some outspoken he-man came along and told Aunt Lavender and my cousin Cosmo where they got off. My only regret is that Uncle Ponsford was not present, so that you could have informed him what you think of his dialect stories. Oh, Walter, do you know that I was seriously considering taking my little hammer and breaking the engagement because you seemed such a poor fish? The way you kept telling Aunt Lavender how much you admired her books and asking her if she worked regular hours or waited for an inspiration. And that hearty laughter of yours every time Uncle Ponsford told the story of the two costermongers who went to Heaven. And your habit of thanking Cosmo for his advice, when the sort of man I wanted to marry would have hit him with a blunt instrument. Can you wonder that I was revolted?'

I felt it only right to put in a word.

'He did it for your sake. He thought you would prefer him not to disembowel your close relatives.'

'Yes, I see that now. My eyes are opened.'

Walter, who had been gulping like a bull-pup trying to swallow a bone too large for its thoracic cavity, contrived to speak.

'Let's get this straight,' he said. 'It is agreed, I think, that I am a fiend in human shape?'

'And by no means the worst of them.'

'But ... and this is where I want you to follow me very closely ... you have no objection to fiends in human shape?'

'Not the slightest.'

'Odd,' said George Porter, who had holed out and joined our

little group, 'most girls dislike them. It was because she considered I was one when I criticized her way of cooking parsnips that there was this rift within the lute between Mabel and myself. Rift within lute all mended now, I am glad to say. She has admitted that she is weak on parsnips. All of which goes to show—'

'You keep out of this, George Porter,' said Walter. He turned to Angela again. 'Then you wouldn't object if we set the joy bells ringing – say a week from next Wednesday?'

'I should enjoy it above all things.'

Walter clasped her to his bosom, using the inter-locking grip, and for some little time they carried on along those lines. Then, gently disengaging herself, she took his arm and led him away. And George Porter and I went off to the clubhouse and split an orange juice.

The rumour, flying to and fro over the London grape-vine, that Stanley Featherstonehaugh Ukridge, that chronically impecunious man of wrath, was going about the metropolis with money on his person found me, when I heard it on my return from a holiday in the country, frankly incredulous. I scoffed at the wild story, even though somebody I met claimed to have met someone else who had actually seen him with the stuff. It was only when I ran into our mutual friend George Tupper in Piccadilly that I began to feel that there might be something in it.

'Ukridge?' said George Tupper. 'Yes, I believe he must have managed to get a little money somehow. I'll tell you why I think so. He called on me this morning when I was in my bath, and when I came out, he had gone. He left, in other words, without trying to extract so much as half-a-crown from me, a thing which has never happened before in the memory of man. But I can't stop now,' said George, who, I noticed, was looking distrait and worried. 'I'm on my way to the police station. I've had a burglary at my place.'

'You don't say?'

'Yes. They rang me up at the club just now. Apparently a suit, a hat, a couple of shirts, some socks, a maroon tie, and a pair of shoes have disappeared.'

'Mysterious.'

'Most. Well, goodbye.'

'Goodbye,' I said, and went off to see Ukridge.

I found him in his bed-sitting room, his feet on the mantel-piece, his pince-nez askew as always, his right hand grasping a refreshing mug of beer.

'Ah, Corky,' he said, waving a welcoming foot. 'Home from your holiday, eh? Brought the roses back to your cheeks, I perceive. I, too, am feeling pretty bobbish. I have just had a great spiritual experience, old horse, which has left me in exalted mood.'

'Never mind your spiritual experiences and your exalted moods. Was it you who pinched George Tupper's hat, suit, socks, shirts, shoes and maroon cravat?'

I make no claim to any particular perspicacity in asking the question. It was pure routine. Whenever suits, shirts, socks, ties and what not are found to be missing, the Big Four at Scotland Yard always begin their investigations by spreading a dragnet for S. F. Ukridge.

He looked pained, as if my choice of verbs had wounded him.

'Pinched, laddie? I don't like that word "pinched". I *borrowed* the objects you mention, yes, for I knew a true friend like old Tuppy would not grudge them to me in my hour of need. I had to have them in order to dazzle this fellow I'm lunching with tomorrow and ensure my securing a job carrying with it a princely salary. He's a pal of my aunt's, this bloke,' – he was alluding to Miss Julia Ukridge, the wealthy novelist – 'and my aunt, learning that he wanted somebody to tutor his son, suggested me. Now that Tuppy has given of his plenty, the thing's in the bag. The tie alone should be enough to put me over.'

'Well, I'm glad you're going to get a job at last, but how the devil can you tutor sons? You don't know enough.'

'I know enough to be able to cope with a piefaced kid of twelve. He'll probably reverence me as one of the world's great minds. Besides, my task, my aunt informs me, will be more to look after the stripling, take him to the British Museum, the Old Vic and so forth, which I can do on my head. Did Tuppy seem at all steamed up about his bereavement?'

'A little, I thought.'

'Too bad. But let me tell you about this great spiritual experience. Do you believe in guardian angels?'

I said I was not sure.

'Then you had better ruddy well be sure,' said Ukridge severely, 'because they exist in droves. Mine is a pippin. He was on the job this afternoon in no uncertain manner, steering me with a loving hand from the soup into which I was on the very verge of plunging. Misled by my advisers, I had supposed the animal couldn't fail to cop.'

'What animal?'

'Dogsbody at Kempton Park.'

'It lost. I saw it in the evening paper.'

'Exactly. That's the point of my story. Let me get the facts in their proper order. Knowing that it was imperative that I be spruce and natty when bursting on this tutor-for-his-son bloke, I hastened to Tuppy's and laid in the necessary supplies. I then went to Wimbledon to see my aunt, she having told me to be on the mat at noon, as she wished to confer with me. And you'll scarcely believe this, old horse, but the first thing she did was to hand me fifteen quid to buy shirts, ties and the rest of it, she having reached the same conclusion as I had about the importance of the outer crust. So there I was, in pocket to the colossal extent of fifteen of the best. And I was just leaving, when Barter sidled up.'

'Barter?'

'My aunt's butler. He sidled up and asked me out of the side of his mouth if I wanted to clean up big. Well, I had already cleaned up big, but every little bit added to what you've got makes just a little bit more, so I bade the honest fellow speak on, and he said, "Put your shirt on Dogsbody at Kempton this afternoon and fear nothing".

'It moved me strangely, Corky. Already someone else – a man I met in a pub – had advised this investment, and Barter, I was aware, knew a bit. He follows form assiduously. Such a tip, coming from such a source, seemed to me sent from heaven and I decided to go a buster and wager my entire assets. My only fear, as I took the next train back to town, was that I might arrive at the offices of my selected bookie too late to put the money on. For the negotiations could not, of course, be conducted over the telephone. I am revealing no secret, Corky, when I say that my credit is not good, and I knew that Jim Simms, the Safe Man, on whom I proposed to bestow my custom, would want cash down in advance.

'The time was about twenty to one when I alighted from the train, and as it was the one o'clock race in which Dogsbody was competing, I had to look slippy. But all seemed well, I reached my destination with five minutes to spare, and I was just about to charge in, clutching the fifteen in my hot hand, when the door opened and out came – of all people – a fellow to whom for the past few years I have owed two pounds, three shillings and sixpence for goods supplied. He recognized me immediately, and I don't think I have ever heard anyone bay more like a bloodhound on the trail of aniseed.

'"Hey!" he cried. "I've been looking for you for years. I would like to take up that matter of my little account, Mr Ukridge."

'Well, there was only one thing to do.'

'Pay him?'

'Of course not. Pay him, indeed! A business man can't fritter away his capital like that, Corky. Strategic retreat seemed to be indicated, and the next moment I was off like a flash, with him after me. And to cut a long story short, when I eventually shook off his challenge, the clocks were pointing to fifteen minutes past one.'

'So you weren't able to back Dogsbody?'

'No. And that is what I meant when I paid that marked tribute to my guardian angel, who obviously arranged the whole thing. I was as sick as mud, of course, at the time, but later, when I saw the evening paper, I realized that this quick-thinking angel had had the situation well in hand, I was extremely grateful to him, and do you know what I'm going to do, Corky? I'm going to give a tithe of that fifteen quid to charity.'

'What!'

'As a sort of thank-offering. I shall go forth into the highways and byways and seek out three deserving cases and slip them each a shilling.'

'Three bob isn't a tithe of fifteen quid.'

'It's as near a tithe as makes no matter.'

'A tithe is a tenth. You ought to give them ten shillings each.'

'Talk sense, old horse,' said Ukridge.

I was late getting home that night for one reason and another, and was shocked when I woke next morning to find what the time was. I should have to move swiftly, I saw. I was supposed to be at the Senior Conservative Club at twelve to interview Horace Wanklyn, the eminent novelist, for the Sunday paper which gave me occasional jobs of that sort, and I knew that eminent novelists purse their lips and tap the floor disapprovingly if the dregs of society like myself keep them waiting.

I had just finished a hurried breakfast and was looking about for the umbrella which I kept for occasions like this – nothing makes a better impression than a tightly rolled umbrella – when Bowles, my ex-butler landlord, accosted me in his majestic way.

'Good morning, sir. Mr Ukridge called shortly after you had left last night.'

He spoke with the tender note in his voice which invariably came into it when he mentioned Ukridge's name. For some reason which I had never been able to understand, he had always had a doglike devotion for that foe of the human species.

'Oh, yes?'

'I gave him the umbrella.'

'Eh?'

'Your umbrella, sir. Mr Ukridge informed me that he wished to borrow it. He desired me to give you his cordial good wishes and to tell you that he expected it – I quote his words – just to turn the scale.'

It was with a hard, set face that I rang Ukridge's front door bell some twenty minutes later. Making the detour to his lair would render me late for Horace Wanklyn, but that could not be helped.

Informed that he was out at the moment, I was turning away, when I saw him coming along the street. He was wearing the Tupper hat, tilted at a jaunty angle, the Tupper suit, socks, shoes and shirt, and was swinging my umbrella like a clouded cane. I had rarely seen anything so dressy.

He listened to my reproaches sympathetically.

'I know just how you feel, Corky. The good man loves his umbrella. But I will take the greatest care of it, and you shall have it back a thousandfold some time this afternoon. What do you want the damn thing for, anyway? It's not raining.'

I explained that I needed it to offset the bagginess of my trousers and the general seediness of my appearance.

'I'm interviewing a big pot at the Senior Conservative Club.'

'You are? Why, that's where I'm lunching with my bloke. Who are you interviewing?'

'Horace Wanklyn, the novelist.'

He seemed stunned.

'Well, upon my Sam, old horse, this is the most amazing coincidence I ever came across in my puff. It's none other than old Pop Wanklyn who is the bird who wants a tutor for his son. My aunt got matey with him at the last Pen and Ink Club dinner. Gosh, the thing is beginning to develop. We must suck profit from this. Here's what you want to do, laddie. Having extracted his views on whatever subject you are proposing to discuss—'

'The Modern Girl.'

'Having heard all he has to spill about the Modern Girl, you say "Oh, by the way, Mr Wanklyn—" ... You don't think you'll be calling him Horace by that time?'

'No, I don't.'

'Mr Wanklyn, then. "Oh, by the way, Mr Wanklyn," you say, "my old friend Ukridge tells me he is lunching with you today, and that you are considering engaging him to ram a bit of education into your ruddy son's ivory skull. You could place the little blister in no better hands. I have known Stanley Ukridge these many years, and I can confidently say—" ... And then a lot of guff which I know I can leave to you. Pitch it strong, Corky. Let the golden words come pouring out like honey. Really, this is an uncanny bit of luck. I had an idea all along that I should reap some reward for that kindly impulse of mine.'

'What kindly ... Oh, you mean the tithe to charity?'

'That's right.'

'When do you start scattering largesse?'

'I have already started. In fact, I've practically finished. Only one deserving case to go now.'

'You've done the other two?'

'Yes. And I don't mind telling you, Corky, that it has left me weak. I hope mine host will not spare the restoratives at lunch, for I need picking up. It was the second deserving case that shattered my aplomb. The first was a cinch. I saw a shabby man standing by a car evidently trying to touch the girl at the wheel. I just walked up, said "Here, my good man", and slipped a bob into his hand, turning away quickly to escape his thanks. But the next one ... !'

Ukridge shivered. He removed George Tupper's hat and mopped his forehead with what I assumed to be one of George Tupper's handkerchiefs.

'Not so good?'

'An ordeal, old horse, nothing less than an ordeal, from which I emerged, as I say, shaken. British Constitution, forsooth!'

'Eh?'

'And She sells sea shells by the sea shore.'

'Are you tight?'

'No, but the cop thought I was.'

'What cop?'

'It's a long story.'

There flitted before my eyes a vision of Horace Wanklyn pacing the floor of the Senior Conservative smoking-room, looking at his watch and muttering 'He cometh not,' but I thrust it from me. However late I might be for the tryst, I had to probe this mystery of cops, British constitutions and sea shells.

'Get on with it,' I said.

Ukridge straightened George Tupper's tie, flicked a speck of dust off the sleeve of George Tupper's coat, and prodded me impressively in the stomach with my umbrella.

'Corky,' he said earnestly, 'the advice I would give to every young man starting out in life is this. If you are going to yield to impulse, be careful before you do so that there isn't a blighter eight feet high and broad in proportion standing behind you. This one, I think, was more like eight feet six.'

'Which one?'

'I'm telling you. At the post office. After slipping the shabby man his shilling, I remembered that I was in need of stamps, so – being well able to afford the expenditure – I strolled to that post office at the corner of the Strand to purchase a few. I went in and found only one customer ahead of me at the stamp counter, a charmingly pretty girl of, I should say, the stenographer class. She was putting in a bid for a couple of twopence-halfpennies and, like all girls, was making quite a production of it. You or I, when we feel the urge for stamps, stride up, ask for them, disgorge the needful and stride away again, but girls like to linger and turn the thing into a social occasion. So as I stood there I had plenty of leisure to look about me and take in the various objects by the wayside. Among them was the girl's handbag, which she had laid on the counter beside her.

'It touched me, laddie. It was one of those pathetic cheap handbags which speak eloquently of honest poverty. Her inexpensive frock also spoke eloquently of honest poverty. So did her hat.'

'We can't all pinch our hats.'

'My heart ached for the poor little thing. I knew exactly what a girl like that would be getting a week. Just about the three or four quid which you or I would spend on a single dinner at the Ritz.'

The idea of Ukridge dining at the Ritz and paying for it took my breath away, and he was able to continue without interruption on my part.

'And I said to myself "Here is where I do my second good deed of the day". But this time, Corky, it was to be no matter of a mere shilling. I proposed to enrich her to the extent of a whole quid.'

'Golly!'

'You may well say "Golly!" But that's me. That is Stanley Ukridge. Lavish, openhanded, not counting the cost where his emotions are stirred. The problem was—'

'How to give it to her?'

'Exactly. You can't go slipping pretty girls to whom you've never been introduced quids. At least, you can, but it may quite easily give rise to misunderstandings. However, I did not have to muse long, for there was a sudden crash outside in the street and the girl legged it to see what was happening, leaving her bag on the counter. To open it and slip in a Treasury note was with me the work of a moment, and I was just stepping back, feeling that this was a far, far better thing than I had ever done, when a heavy hand fell on my shoulder and there was this eight-feet-six bird. All unknown to me he had lined up behind me in the queue, and I could see at a glance that he was one of those public-minded good citizens who cause so much trouble.

'With a curt "Gotcher!" he led me out into the street. Resistance was hopeless. The muscles of his brawny arms were strong as iron bands.

' "Is this your bag, madam?" he asked the girl, who was standing drinking in the wreckage of a couple of taxis. "I caught this man pilfering its contents. Constable!" said the eight-feet-sixer, addressing the rozzer who was presiding over the scene of the accident, and the rozzer came up.

'Well, there was nothing for it now, of course, but to outline the facts. I did so, and my story was sceptically received. I could see they found it thin. Fortunately at this point the girl, who had been checking up on the bag, uttered a sharp squeal and reported that she was a quid ahead of the game, so my innocence was established.

'But not my sobriety. These rozzers don't understand pure altruism. When they find someone shoving quids into the handbags of perfect strangers, only one solution occurs to them. Mercifully, it being earlyish in the day and me rather saving myself up for that lunch with Horace Wanklyn, when I would be able to get it free, it happened that I had not partaken of alcoholic refreshment since the previous night, so when at his request I breathed on the constable, all he drew was the aroma of coffee and eggs and bacon, and it seemed to me that I had shaken him.

'But these cops don't give up easily. They fight to the last ditch. I was compelled to utter in a clear voice the words "British Constitution" and "She sells sea shells by the sea shore" and in addition to walk a chalk line obligingly drawn on the pavement by the eight-feet-sixer, who since the girl's revelation had been showing a nasty spirit like that of a tiger cheated of its prey. And it is extremely humiliating for a proud man, Corky, to have to say "She sells sea shells by the sea shore" and walk a chalk line in front of a large crowd. When at long last I was permitted to pop off, my nervous system was in a state of hash, and the whole episode has left me with the feeling that my next good deed, the concluding one of the series, has got to be an easy one, or I give it a miss.'

It proved to be quite an easy one. Even as he spoke, there came shuffling along a ragged individual badly in need of a shave. I saw his eye light up as it fell on the splendour of Ukridge's costume. He asked Ukridge if he felt inclined to save a human life, and Ukridge said yes, if it could be done for sixpence. The ragged individual assured him that sixpence would be ample, it being bread that he was in need of. He had not, he said, tasted bread for some considerable time, and sixpence-worth would set him up nicely.

The money changed hands, and I was a little surprised by the effusiveness of the recipient's gratitude. He pawed Ukridge all over like a long-lost brother. I would not have supposed myself that sixpence justified all that emotion, but if you are fond of bread, no doubt you look on these things from a different angle.

'Touching,' said Ukridge, alluding to this osteopathic exhibition.

'Very touching.'

'Still, that lets me out. From now on, to hell with the deserving poor! You off?'

'You bet I'm off. I'm twenty minutes late already.'

And I set a course for the Senior Conservative Club in Northumberland Avenue.

It was a relief to find on arriving at journey's end that the party of the second part had not yet shown up at the tryst. I was accommodated with a seat in the hall, and after another quarter of an hour, pleasantly spent in watching Senior Conservatives flit by *en route* for the trough, I saw the hall porter pointing me out to a man in a glistening top hat who had just come in. From the fact that he headed in my direction I deduced that this must be the author of that series of powerful novels which plumbed the passionate heart of Woman and all that sort of thing and rendered him in consequence an ideal set-up for an interview on the Modern Girl.

'Mr Er-Ah? From the *Sunday Dispatch*? How do you do? I hope you have not been waiting long? I am a little late. I – er – I had to go home for something.'

Horace Wanklyn was a long, thin, stringy man in the early fifties with a long, thin, stringy neck concealed at the moment behind the highest collar I had ever seen on human shirt. It seemed to be giving him a certain amount of discomfort, for he wriggled a good deal, and I thought he seemed ill at ease in the morning coat and striped trousers which completed his costume. But there was no gainsaying their effectiveness as a spectacle. Solomon in all his glory and Ukridge in George Tupper's herring-bone double-breasted grey tweed with the custom-made lapels had nothing on this superbly upholstered man of letters.

I said I would appreciate it if he told me how he felt about the Modern Girl, and his eyes lit up as if he were glad I had asked him that. He sat down and began to talk, and right from the start it became evident that he took an extremely dim view of the Modern Girl. He resented her bossiness, her determination to have her own way, her lack of proper respect for her elders and her habit of keeping on and on about a thing like – I quote his words, as Bowles would have said – a damned governess.

'Nag, nag, nag!' said Horace Wanklyn, plainly brooding on some episode in his past of which I knew nothing.

'Nag, nag, nag, nag, nag!'

It was after he had spoken for perhaps ten minutes, giving me a wealth of rich material for my column and a quarter, that he paused and looked at me intently.

'You married?'

I said I was not.

'No daughters?'

'No daughters.'

'Ah!' It seemed to me that he sighed a little enviously. 'I see you're wearing a soft shirt.'

'Yes.'

'With a soft collar.'

'Yes.'

'And grey flannel trousers, baggy at the knees.'

'Yes.'

'Lucky young devil!' said Horace Wanklyn.

As he spoke, a young man came in from the street and started to cross the hall. Catching sight of my companion, he halted, spellbound.

'Golly, Uncle Horace!' he exclaimed. 'You look like Great Lovers Through The Ages. What's the idea of the fancy dress? Why are you disguised as a gentleman today?'

Horace Wanklyn sighed heavily.

'Patricia made me go home and put them on.'

'Your child? Your daughter Patricia?'

'She and her sister have been after me for months about the way I dressed.'

'And rightly.'

'It isn't rightly at all.' Horace Wanklyn stirred uneasily, whether from annoyance or because the corner of his collar had jabbed him in the neck I was unable to say. 'Why shouldn't I dress comfortably? I'm not a Duke. I'm not an Ambassador. I'm a literary man. Look at this young fellow, who is also a literary man. Soft shirt, soft collar and baggy flannel trousers. Look at Balzac. He used to wear a monk's robe. Look at—'

'I can't look at anything but you. I'm fascinated. But aren't those things you're wearing comfortable?'

'Of course they're not comfortable. I'm suffering agonies. But I had to put them on. Patricia and her sister insisted,' said Horace Wanklyn, and I thought what a good sentence that would have been for the constable to have used on Ukridge. 'Patricia drove me here in the car, nagging the whole way, and I had just got out and she was saying that if I persisted in going about looking like one of the submerged tenth, someone was going to come up to me and say "Here, my good man" and give me a shilling, when I'm dashed if someone *didn't* come up to me and say "Here, my good man" and give me a shilling.'

'Right on cue.'

'Yes,' said Horace Wanklyn, and brooded for a moment in silence. 'Well, you can guess the sequel,' he resumed, having passed a finger round the inside of his collar in the apparent hope of loosening it. 'Patricia said "There!" – you know how women say "There!" – and the long and the short of it was that I was compelled to go home and change into these damned things.'

'You look lovely.'

'I know I look lovely, but I can't breathe.'

'Do you want to?'

'Certainly I want to. And I'll tell you another thing I want' – here Horace Wanklyn gritted his teeth and there came into his eyes a cold, purposeful gleam – 'and that is some day, somewhere, to meet that "Here, my good man" fellow again and deal with him faithfully. The idea I have in mind is to cut him into small pieces with a rusty knife.'

'Having first sprinkled him with boiling oil?'

'Yes,' said Horace Wanklyn, weighing the suggestion and evidently approving of it. 'Having first sprinkled him with boiling oil, I shall then dance on his remains.' He turned to me. 'There is nothing more I can tell you, Mr Er-Ah?'

'Not a thing, thanks.'

'Then I'll be getting along to the coffee-room and booking a table. I'm lunching with a nephew of Julia Ukridge's,' he explained to the young man.

There I thought he was being too optimistic – or, it might be better to say pessimistic. I had a feeling that when I had conveyed to him the substance of the recent conversation, Ukridge might deem it the prudent course to absent himself from the feast. Ukridge had always been a good trencherman, particularly when a guest, but it spoils the most lavish meal if your host starts sprinkling you with boiling oil and cutting you into small pieces.

And I was right. As I waited in the street outside the club, he came bustling up.

'Hullo, old horse. Finished your interview?'

'Yes,' I said. 'And you've finished your lunch.'

As he listened to the story I had to tell, his mobile features gradually lengthened. A lifetime of reeling beneath the slings and arrows of outrageous Fortune had left this man's fibres toughened, but not so toughened that he was able to bear the latest of them with nonchalance.

However, after we had walked some little distance, he seemed to rally.

'Ah, well,' he said. '*Oh, ever thus from childhood's hour I've seen my fondest hopes decay. I never loved a tree or flower but 'twas the first to fade away.* I always remember those lines, Corky, having had to write them out five hundred times on the occasion at school when I brought a stink bomb into the form-room. The son-tutoring job would appear to be off.'

'If I read aright the message in Horace Wanklyn's eyes, yes.'

'On the other hand, I've got this colossal sum of fifteen ... no, it's a bit less than that now, isn't it? ... this colossal sum of ...

perhaps I'd better count it.' He reached for his hip-pocket, and his jaw fell like a drooping lily. 'Corky! My wallet's gone!'

'What!'

'I see it all. It was that blister I gave the sixpence to. You remember how he pawed me?'

'I remember. You were touched.'

'Touched,' said Ukridge in a hollow voice, 'is right.'

A ragged individual came up. London seemed full of ragged individuals today. He took a brief look at the knees of my trousers, dismissed me as having ore-producing potentialities and transferred his attention to Ukridge.

'Pardon me addressing you, sir, but am I right in supposing that you are Captain the Honourable Anthony Wilberforce?'

'No.'

'You are not Captain the Honourable Anthony Wilberforce?'

'No.'

'You *look* very like Captain the Honourable Anthony Wilberforce.'

'I can't help that.'

'I'm sorry you are not Captain the Honourable Anthony Wilberforce, because he is a very liberal, open-handed gentleman. If I had told Captain the Honourable Anthony Wilberforce that it is some considerable time since I tasted bread—'

'Come on, Corky!' said Ukridge.

The love feast was over. Deserving Poor Ordinaries were down in the cellar, with no takers.

Conversations were in progress in the smoking room of the Drones with a view to making up a party to go and see the Wrestling Championship at the Albert Hall, and a Bean suggested that Oofy Prosser be invited to join the expedition. Oofy, he put it to the meeting, had more pimples than the man of taste liked to be seen about with and was perhaps the nearest approach to a piece of cheese which the human race had so far produced, but he possessed one outstanding merit which went far to counter-balance these defects – viz. a stupendous bank account, and it was quite conceivable that, if handled right, he might loosen up and stand supper after the performance.

The proposal was well received, and when Oofy entered a few moments later the Bean issued his invitation. To the general surprise, instead of seeming gratified by this demand for his society, the club millionaire recoiled with every evidence of loathing and horror. At the mention of the word 'wrestling' a look of intense malevolence passed over his face.

'Wrestling?' he cried. 'You ask me to spend good money on a wrestling match? You want me to pay out cash to witness the obscene gyrations of a couple of pot-bellied nitwits who fritter away their time wallowing on mats and behaving like lunatic osteopaths? Wrestlers, forsooth! The scum of the earth! I'd like to dig a hole in the ground and collect all the wrestlers in the world and dump them into it, having previously skinned them with a blunt knife and cooked them over a slow fire. Wrestlers, indeed. Bah! Pah! Faugh! Tchah!' said Oofy Prosser, and turned on his heel and left the room.

An Egg was the first to break the puzzled silence.

'Do you know what I think?' he said. 'I don't believe Oofy likes wrestlers.'

'Exactly the thought that occurred to me, reading between the lines,' agreed the Bean.

'You are perfectly right,' said a Crumpet. 'Your intuition has not deceived you. I was about to warn you, when he came in. He was recently interested in a venture connected with wrestlers and lost quite a bit of money. And you know how Oofy feels about parting with money.'

His hearers nodded. In matters of finance their clubmate's dogged adhesiveness was a byword. Not one of those present but in his time had endeavoured to dip into the Prosser millions, always without success.

'That's why he isn't speaking to Freddie Widgeon now. It was through him that he got mixed up in the thing. Owing to Freddie, Jas Waterbury entered Oofy's life. And once Jas Waterbury enters your life, Freddie tells me, you can kiss at least a portion of your holdings good-bye.

'I wonder if I have happened to mention this Jas Waterbury to you before. Did I tell you about the time when Freddie sang at that Amateur Night binge down in Bottleton East and was accompanied on the piano by a greasy bird whom he had picked up in the neighbourhood? I did? Well, that was Jas Waterbury. In a brawl in a pub later on in the evening, Freddie happened to save his life, and on the strength of this he has been rolling up to the club and touching his brave preserver ever since for sums ranging from sixpence to as much as half a crown.

'You would think that if Bloke A saves Bloke B's life, it ought to be the former who touches the latter and not vice versa, but the *noblesse oblige* of the Widgeons does not permit Freddie to see it that way. He recognizes Jas Waterbury's claim and continues to brass up.'

The chain of events with which my narrative deals (proceeded the Crumpet) started to uncoil itself, or whatever chains do, about a month ago. It was on a breezy morning towards the middle of May that Freddie, emerging from the club, found Jas Waterbury lurking on the steps. A couple of bob changed hands, and Freddie was about to shift on, when the other froze on to his coat sleeve and detained him.

'Half a mo, cocky,' said Jas Waterbury. 'Do you want to make a packet?' And Freddie, who has been hoping to make a packet since he was sacked from his first kindergarten, replied that Jas Waterbury interested him strangely.

'That's the way to talk,' said the greasy bird. 'That's the spirit I like to see. Well, I can ease you in on the ground floor of the biggest thing since the Mint. Just slip me a couple of hundred quid for working expenses and we're off.'

Freddie laughed a hollow, mirthless laugh. The only time he had ever had money like that in his possession was when his uncle, Lord Blicester, had given him his wallet to hold while he brushed his topper.

'A couple of hundred quid?' he said. 'Gosh, Jas Waterbury, from the light-hearted way you speak of such sums one would think you thought I was Oofy Prosser.'

'Oofy how much?'

'Prosser. The wealthiest bimbo in the Drones. Silk underwear, shoes by Lobb, never without a flower in the buttonhole, covered with pimples, each pimple produced by gallons of vintage champagne, and always with an unsightly bulge in his breast pocket, where he keeps his roll. Ask him for your couple of hundred quids, my misguided old chunk of grease, not a poor deadbeat who is pretty shortly going to find a difficulty in getting his three square a day, unless the ravens do their stuff.'

And he was starting to biff off, with another sardonic laugh at the idea of anyone mistaking him for a plutocrat, when Jas Waterbury uttered these momentous words.

'Well, why don't you slip me an intro to this gentleman friend of yours? Then, if he puts up the splosh, you get a commish.'

Freddie stared at him with bulging eyes. If you had told him half an hour before that the moment would come when he would look upon Jas Waterbury and find him almost beautiful, he would have scouted the idea. But this was what was happening now.

'A commish?' he whispered. 'Golly, now you're talking. We'll go round and see him now. What's the time? Half past eleven? We ought to catch him at breakfast.'

Their mission proved a complete success. I was at the bar next morning, having one for the tonsils, when Oofy blew in, and from the fact that his eyes were aglow and his pimples gleaming, I deduced that he had spotted a chance of making money. In repose, as you know, Oofy's eyes are like those of a dead fish, but if he thinks he sees a way of adding to his disgustingly large bank balance, they glitter with a strange light.

'I say,' he said, 'do you know anything about wrestling? Professional wrestling, I mean. The all-in stuff. Good box-office value, isn't it?'

I said that I had always understood so, especially up North.

'So this chap Waterbury says. Yesterday,' explained Oofy, 'Freddie Widgeon brought a fellow named Waterbury to see me, and he placed a proposition before me which looks dashed good. It seems that he knows a couple of all-in wrestlers, and he wants me to advance two hundred quid for working capital, the scheme being that we hire a hall in one of these Northern manufacturing towns and put these birds on and clean up. He says we can safely bill the thing as a European championship, because nobody up there is going to know if a wrestler is a champion or not. Then we have a return match, and after that the rubber match, and then we start all over again somewhere else. There ought to be a pot of money in it.'

My heart was heavy at the thought of Oofy making more money, but I had to agree. Such a series of contests, I felt, could scarcely fail to bring home the bacon. Blood in these Northern manufacturing towns is always very rich and sporting, and it was practically a certainty that the inhabitants would amble up in their thousands.

'I'm going down to a pub at Barnes this afternoon to have a look at the fellows. From what Waterbury tells me, there seems no doubt that they are the goods. I shall probably make a fortune. There is the purse, of course, and Waterbury's cut, and I'm paying Freddie a ten per cent commission, but even so the profits ought to be enormous.'

He licked his lips, and feeling that this might possibly be my moment, I asked him if he could lend me a fiver till Wednesday. He said No, he ruddy well could not, and the episode closed.

At two o'clock that afternoon, Oofy bowled down in his princely sports model two-seater to the White Stag, Barnes, and at twenty to three, Jas Waterbury, looking greasier than ever, was introducing him to the two catch-as-catch-canners.

It was a breath-taking experience. His first emotion, he tells me, was one of surprise that so much human tonnage could have been assembled in one spot. A cannibal king, beholding them, would have whooped with joy and reached for his knife and fork with the feeling that for once the catering department had not failed him; and if you could have boiled them down for tallow, you would have had enough ha'penny dips to light the homes of all the residents of Barnes for about a year and a quarter.

Reading from left to right, the pair consisted of an obese bounder who looked like a gorilla which has been doing itself too well on the bananas and a second obese bounder who would have made a hippopotamus seem streamlined. They had small, glittering eyes, no foreheads and more hair all over than you would have believed possible.

Jas Waterbury did the honours.

'Mr Porky Jupp and Mr Plug Bosher.'

The Messrs Jupp and Bosher said they were pleased to meet Oofy, but Oofy wasn't so sure he could look at the thing from the same kindly angle. The thought crossed his mind that if, when walking down a lonely alley on a moonless night, he had had to meet two of his fellow men, these were the two he would have picked last. Their whole personalities gave him the impression that neither was safe off the chain.

This conviction grew as he watched the exhibition bout which they put on for his benefit. It was like witnessing a turn-up between two pluguglies of the Stone Age. They snorted and gurgled and groaned and grunted and rolled on each other and jumped on each other and clutched each other's throats and bashed each other's faces and did the most extraordinary things to each other's stomachs. The mystery to Oofy was that they didn't come unstuck.

When the orgy scene was over, he was pale beneath his pimples and panting like a stag at bay, but convinced beyond the possibility of doubt that this was the stuff to give the rugged dwellers up North. As soon as he could get his breath back, he informed Jas Waterbury that he would write out a cheque immediately: and this having been done, they parted; Jas Waterbury and the almost humans leaving for a cottage in the country, where the latter could conduct their training out of reach of the temptations of the great city, and Oofy tooling home in the two-seater with the comfortable feeling that in the not distant future his current account would be swelling up as if it had got dropsy.

It had been Oofy's original intention, partly in order to keep a fatherly eye on his investment and partly because he wanted to watch the mass murderers pirouetting on each other's stomachs again, to look in at the training camp pretty shortly. But what with one thing and another, he didn't seem able to get around to it, and a couple of weeks passed with him still infesting the metrop.

However, he presumed Jas Waterbury was carrying on all right. He pictured Jas sweating away in and around the cottage, not sparing himself, a permanent blot on the rural scene. It surprised him, accordingly, when one morning Freddie Widgeon came into the Club and told him that the blighter was waiting in the hall.

'Looking dashed solemn and sinister,' said Freddie. 'His manner, as he touched me for two bob, was strange and absent. I say, you don't think anything's gone wrong with the works, do you?'

This was precisely what Oofy was thinking. The presence of this greasy bird in Dover Street, W., when he should have been slithering about in the depths of the country, put him into a twitter. He legged it to the hall, followed by Freddie, and found Jas Waterbury chewing a dead cigar and giving the club appointments an approving once over.

'Nice little place you've got here. Pip, pip,' said Jas Waterbury. Oofy was in no mood for chit-chat.

'Never mind about my nice little place. What about your nice little place? Why aren't you at the cottage with the thugs?'

'Exactly,' said Freddie. 'Your place is at their side.'

'Well, the fact is, cockies,' said Jas Waterbury, 'an awkward situation has arisen, and I thought we ought to have a conference. They've gone and had a quarrel. There's been a rift within the lute, if you understand the expression, and it looks as if it was spreading.'

Oofy could make nothing of this. Nor could Freddie. Oofy asked what the dickens that mattered, and Freddie asked what the dickens that mattered, too.

'I'll tell you what it matters, cockies,' said Jas Waterbury, putting his cigar gravely behind his ear and looking like a chunk of margarine with a secret sorrow. 'Unless we can heal the rift, ruin stares us in the eyeball.' And in a few crisp words he explained the inwardness of the situation.

Professional wrestling, it seems, is a highly delicate and scientific business which you can't just bung into a haphazard spirit, relying for your effects on the inspiration of the moment. Aggravated acts of mayhem like those perpetrated by Porky Jupp and Plug Bosher come to flower only after constant rehearsal, each move, down to the merest gnashing of the teeth, being carefully thought out in the quiet seclusion of the study and polished to the last button with unremitting patience. Otherwise the thing doesn't look right, and audiences complain.

Obviously, then, what you require first and foremost in a

couple of wrestlers whom you are readying for the arena, is a mutual sympathy and a cordial willingness to collaborate. And until recently such a sympathy had existed between Porky Jupp and Plug Bosher in abundant measure, each helping each and working unselfishly together for the good of the show.

To give them an instance of what he meant, said Jas Waterbury, Porky would come along one day, after musing apart for a while, and suggest that Plug should sock him on the nose, because it would be a swell effect and he never felt anything when socked on the nose except a rather agreeable tickling sensation. Upon which, Plug, not to be outdone in the courtesies, would place his stomach unreservedly at the other's disposal, inviting him to jump up and down on it to his heart's content; he having so much stomach that he scarcely noticed it if people did buck-and-wings on the outskirts.

'Just a couple of real good pals,' said Jas Waterbury, 'like what's-his-name and who-was-it in the Bible. It was beautiful to see their team work. But now they've come over all nasty, and what's to be what I might call the upshot is more than I can tell you. If there hadn't been this rift within the lute, we'd have had a fine, stirring performance full of entertainment value and one long thrill from start to finish, but if they're going to be cross with each other, it won't look like anything. It'll all be over in a couple of minutes, because Plug can always clean up Porky with one hand if he wants to. And then what? People throwing pop bottles and yelling "Fake!"'

'Well, that won't matter,' said Oofy, pointing out the bright side. 'They'll already have paid for their seats.'

'And what about the return match? And the rubber match? If the first show's a flop, it'll get around and we'll be playing to empty benches.'

They saw what he was driving at now, and Freddie, all of a doodah at the prospect of losing his commish, uttered a low cry and sucked feverishly at the knob of his umbrella. As for Oofy, a look of anguish passed over his face, leaping from pimple to pimple like the chamois of the Alps from crag to crag, and he asked how far the breach had widened. Were relations between these two garrotters really so very strained?

'Well, they're still speaking to each other.'

'That's good.'

'No, that's bad,' corrected Jas Waterbury. 'Because every time they open their mouths, it's to make a dirty crack. I tell you, if you want to see your money back, you'd better come and try and reason with them.'

Oofy said his two-seater was at the door, and they would start at once. Freddie wanted to come, too, but Oofy wouldn't let him. When you're all in a dither, with ruin staring you in the eyeball, you don't want to be hampered by Freddie Widgeon. Jas Waterbury asked Freddie if he could lend him a couple of bob, and Freddie said he had lent him a couple of bob, and Jas Waterbury said Oh sorry, he had forgotten, and didn't that just show what a state of mind he was in? He and Oofy popped off.

To say that Oofy was all in a dither is really to give too feeble a picture of his emotions. They were such that only a top-notcher like Shakespeare could have slapped them down on paper, and he would have had to go all out.

What made his head swim was the mystery of the thing. Here were a couple of birds who for years had apparently been two minds with but a single thought, and their ancient friendship had suddenly taken the knock. Why? For what reason? He sought in vain for a reply.

It seemed hours before they got to journey's end. When they did, a single glance was enough to show Oofy that Jas Waterbury knew a rift within the lute when he saw one. The two gorillas were plainly on the chilliest of terms. And when he watched them wrestle, he saw exactly what Jas had meant.

All the spirit had gone out of the thing. Plug Bosher still socked Porky Jupp on the nose, but coldly and formally, and when Porky jumped on Plug's stomach it was with a frigid aloofness which, if exhibited before a paying audience, must inevitably have brought out the pop bottles like hailstones.

Oofy stayed on to dinner, and when it was over and Plug and Porky had gone off to bed without saying good-night to one another, Jas Waterbury looked at him with despondency written all over his greasy face. It was obvious that only the fact of his having no soul prevented the iron entering into it.

'You see. Not a hope.'

But Oofy had perked up amazingly. His quick intelligence had enabled him by now to spot the root of the trouble. When there is money in the offing, Oofy thinks like lightning.

'Not at all,' he replied. 'Tails up, Jas Waterbury. The sun is still shining.'

Jas Waterbury said he didn't see any ruddy sun, and Oofy said possibly not, but it was there all right and would shortly come smiling through.

'The thing is quite simple, I was on to it in a second directly we started dinner, if you can call it dinner. All that has happened is that these two bounders have got dyspepsia.'

His companion's eyebrows rose, and he uttered a sharp 'Gor-blimey!' Whoever heard of wrestlers getting dyspepsia, he asked incredulously, adding that he had once known one who lived on pickled pig's trotters and ice cream, washing the mixture down with sparkling limado, a beverage to which he was greatly attached.

'And, what's more, throve on it. Blossomed like a rose in June.'

'Quite,' said Oofy. 'No doubt wrestlers can eat almost anything. Nevertheless, there is a point beyond which the human stomach, be it even that of a wrestler, cannot be pushed, and that point has been reached – nay, passed – in this establishment. The meal of which we have just partaken was the sort of meal an inexperienced young female buzzard might have prepared for her newly married buzzard husband. When I was a boy, I had a goat that ate brass door knobs. That goat would have passed up tonight's steak with a dainty shudder of distaste. Who does the cooking in this joint? Lucrezia Borgia?'

'A woman comes from the village.'

'Then tell her to go back to the village and jolly well stay there, and I'll look in at a good agency tomorrow and get somebody who knows how to cook. You'll soon see the difference. Porky Jupp will become all smiles, and Plug Bosher will skip like the high hills. A week from now I confidently expect to find them chewing each other's ears and bashing each other's noses with all the old mateyness and camaraderie.'

Jas Waterbuy said he believed Oofy was right, and Oofy said he bally well knew he was right.

'Cor! Chase my Aunt Fanny up a gum tree!' cried Jas, infected with his enthusiasm. 'You knew something when you said the blinking sun would soon be shining through the blinking clouds, because there it is, all alive-o. But you needn't go to any agencies and be skinned for fees. I'll send for my niece.'

'Have you a niece?' said Oofy, sorry for the unfortunate girl.

'I have three nieces,' said Jas Waterbury, with a touch of the smugness of the man of property. 'This one's in service as kitchen maid in Green Street, Mayfair. She does for the family when the cook's out, and never fails to give satisfaction.'

Oofy, thinking it over, could see no objection to engaging this Myrtle Cootes, for such, it appeared, was her name. Mayfair kitchen maids, he knew, were always red-hot stuff with the roasts and boileds, and he shared his companion's dislike for paying fees. So it was arranged that on his return to the metrop he should call on her with a letter of introduction explaining the circs, and bright and early on the following morning he did so.

Myrtle Cootes proved to be very much the sort of niece you would have expected a man like Jas Waterbury to have. In features and expression she resembled a dead codfish on a slab. She wore steel-rimmed spectacles, topping them off with ginger hair and adenoids. But Oofy wasn't looking for a Venus de Milo or a Helen of Troy: what he wanted was a Grade A skillet wielder, and a private word with the cook assured him that the culinary arrangements of the training camp could safely be placed in this gargoyle's hands. The cook said she had taught Myrtle Cootes all she knew, and produced testimonials from former employers to show that what she knew was practically the whole art of dinner-dishing from soup to toothpicks.

So Myrtle was instructed to get in touch with the front office and explain that she was obliged to leave immediately owing to sickness at home, and next day Oofy drove her down to the cottage with her corded box and her adenoids and left her there. He stayed on to lunch to get a flash of her form, and was more than satisfied with the girl's virtuosity. She gave them a nourishing soup of the type that sticks to the ribs and puts hair on the chest, followed by a steak and kidney pie with two veg. and a roly-poly pudding with raisins in it, and the stuff fairly melted in their mouths.

The effect of these improved browsing conditions on the two mastodons was instantaneous and gratifying. They downed their soup as if in a roseate dream, and scarcely had the echoes died away when there was another sloshing sound as the milk of human kindness came surging back into them.

By the time the roly-poly pudding with raisins in it had gone down the hatch, all disagreement and unpleasantness had been forgotten. They beamed at each other with the old cordiality. Plug Bosher's voice, as he asked Porky Jupp to reach him the bread, would have passed anywhere for that of a turtle-dove cooing to its mate, and so would Porky Jupp's when he said, 'Right ho, cully, here she comes.' Oofy was so enchanted that he actually went into the kitchen and gave Myrtle Cootes a treasury note for ten bob. And when Oofy voluntarily separates himself from ten bob, you can be pretty sure that his whole being has been stirred to its foundations.

It was on his way home that it suddenly occurred to him that he could set the seal on the day's good work by easing Freddie Widgeon out of the deal and so relieving the venture of the burden of that ten per cent commish of his. Right from the start the thought of having to slip Freddie ten per cent of the profits had been like a dagger in his heart. So when he met him in the club that night and Freddie began bleating for the lowdown on conditions at the front, he shoved on a look of alarm and despondency and told him that the whole thing was a wash-out. The rift between the two principals, he said, had got such a toe-hold that it was hopeless to attempt a reconciliation, and so, seeing no sense in going ahead and getting the bird from a slavering mob of infuriated Yorkshiremen, he had decided to cancel the whole project.

And when, as was natural, this caused Freddie to Oh-death-where-is-thy-sting a goodish bit, Oofy laid an affectionate hand on his shoulder and said he knew exactly how he felt.

'It's the thought of you that's been worrying me into a fever, Freddie old man. I know how you were looking forward to cleaning up with that ten per of yours. The first thing I said to myself was, "I mustn't let good old Freddie down." Well, it's a trifle, of course, to what you would have made, but I'm going to give you a tenner. Yes, yes, I insist. Just scribble me a line as a matter of form, saying that you accept this in full settlement of all claims, and we'll be straight.'

Freddie did so with a tear of gratitude in his eye, and that was that.

In the days that followed I doubt if you could have met a chirpier millionaire than Oofy Prosser. He came into the club whistling, he hummed as he sauntered to and fro, and once, when at the bar, actually burst into song. And when Freddie, who happened to be in the bar at the time, expressed surprise at this jauntiness, he explained that he was merely wearing the mask.

'One must be British. The stiff upper lip, what?'

'Oh, rather,' said Freddie.

Nor did Jas Waterbury's bulletins from the training camp do anything to diminish his exuberance. Jas Waterbury wrote that everything was going like a breeze. Brotherly love was getting stronger on the wing daily. Porky Jupp had suggested that when he jumped on Plug Bosher's stomach Plug Bosher should bite him in the ankle, and Plug Bosher had said he would be charmed to do so, only Porky Jupp must bite him on the nose. Jas Waterbury said that Oofy was missing something in not being there to taste Myrtle's Irish stew, and added that Plug Bosher had put on another inch around the waist.

So rosy was the picture he drew that Oofy, after singing in the bar, went and sang in the hall, and those who were present said that they had never heard anything more carefree. Catsmeat Potter-Pirbright, in particular, compared it to the trilling of a nightingale. There is no question that at this juncture Oofy Prosser was sitting on top of the world.

It was consequently a shattering shock to him when Jas Waterbury's telegram arrived. Strolling into the club one afternoon with a song on his lips and finding a telegram for him in the 'P' box, he opened it idly, with no premonition of an impending doom, and a moment later was feeling as if Porky Jupp had jumped on his stomach.

'Come running, cocky,' wired his business associate, careful even in the stress of what was evidently a powerful emotion to keep it down to twelve words. 'Another rift within lute. Ruin stares eyeball. Regards. Waterbury.'

I described Oofy's state of mind on his previous visit to the camp, if you remember, as dithery. It would be difficult to find an adjective capable of handling his emotions now. That telegram had got right in amongst him and churned him up good and proper.

He had been so sure that there would be no more unfortunate incidents and that he would soon be beaming through the grill at his receiving teller and drinking in the man's low whistle of respectful astonishment as he noted the figures on the cheque he was depositing. And now . . . It began to look to him as though there were a curse on this enterprise of his.

It was getting on for the quiet evenfall when he fetched up at the cottage. The air was cool and fragrant, and the declining sun, doing its stuff in and about the garden, lit up the trees and the little lawn. On the lawn he observed Porky Jupp plucking the petals from a daisy and heard, as he hurried past, his muttered, 'She loves me, she loves me not'; while a short distance away, Plug Bosher, armed with a pocket knife, was carving on a tree a heart with an arrow through it. Neither appeared aware of the other's existence.

In the doorway stood Jas Waterbury, moodily regarding the pair. His sombre face lightened a little as he perceived Oofy, and he drew him into the house.

'You saw them, cocky?' he said. 'You took a good gander at them? Then there's no need for me to explain. That picture tells the story.'

Oofy, recoiling, for the other was breathing heavily in his face and the first thing the man of sensibility does when Jas Waterbury breathes in his face is to recoil as far as possible, replied with some asperity that there was every need for him to explain. And Jas Waterbury said had he observed the daisy? Had he noticed the heart with the arrow through it? He had? Well, there you are, then.

'They're rivals in love, cocky, that's what's happened. They've both of 'em gone and got mushy on Myrtle.'

You could have knocked Oofy down with a feather. The thing didn't seem to him to make sense. With a strong effort he succeeded in steadying his brain, which was going round in circles like a performing mouse. He stared at Jas Waterbury.

'With Myrtle?'

'That's right.'

Oofy still found himself unable to grasp the gist. He stared harder than ever.

'With Myrtle?' he repeated. 'Here, let's get this straight. You say these two blisters love Myrtle? The Cootes disaster, you mean? You are not speaking of some other Myrtle? Your reference is to the slab-faced human codfish in the kitchen?'

Jas Waterbury drew himself up with a touch of pique.

'I'd call Myrtle a nice-looking girl.'

'I wouldn't.'

'She's supposed to look like me.'

'That's what I mean,' said Oofy. 'You must have got your facts twisted. Why would anyone fall in love with Myrtle?'

'Well, there's her cooking.'

For the first time Oofy began to find the thing credible. Himself a greedy hog, he could appreciate the terrific force of the impact of Myrtle Cootes's cooking on two men whose meals had previously been prepared by the woman who came in from the village. Fellows like Porky Jupp and Plug Bosher, he reminded himself, are practical. They do not seek for the softer feminine graces. Overlooking codfish faces and adenoids, they allow their affections to be ensnared by the succulent steak, the cunningly handled veg., the firm, white, satisfying roly-poly pudding with raisins in it. Beauty fades, but these things remain.

'But this is frightful!' he yipped.

'Bad enough for me,' assented Jas Waterbury. 'They've got the idea that she thinks wrestling ungentlemanly, and they're considering chucking it and going in for something else. I heard Plug ask her yesterday if she could love a copper's nark, and I've seen Porky reading a correspondence course advertisement about how to make a large fortune breeding Angora rabbits. If you ask me if the outlook's black, I reply, "Yes, cocky, blacker that Plug Bosher's nails." I see no future in the racket.'

At these words of doom, Oofy tottered to the window. He needed air. Looking out, he saw that Porky Jupp had finished plucking the petals of his daisy. He had crossed the lawn to where Plug Bosher was carving the heart on the tree and was gazing on his handiwork with an unpleasant sneer. He said nothing, but there was a quiet contempt in his manner which was plainly affecting the other like a bad notice in the Art section of the *Spectator*. With a sullen scowl Plug Bosher closed his pocket knife and walked away.

'See?' said Jas Waterbury. 'That's the way they go on all the time now. Rivals in love.'

'Which one of them does she like?' asked Oofy dully.

'She doesn't like either of 'em. I keep telling them that, but they won't believe me. You can't drive reason into a wrestler's nut. Porky says there's something in the way she looks at him which convinces him that he could put it over if only Plug wasn't always messing around; and Plug says you've only got to listen to the girl's quick breathing when he comes along to see that the thing's in the bag; only every time he's just going to pour out his heart, he steps on something and it's Porky. They're vain. That's what's the trouble with them. I've never met an all-in wrestler that didn't think he was Clark Gable. But listen, cocky, I've got an idea.'

'I'll bet it's rotten.'

'It isn't any such thing. It's a pip. It came to me like a flash while we were talking. Suppose somebody was to come along and cut both of 'em out. See what I mean? The handsome man about town from the city.'

Oofy had not expected to be impressed by any suggestion of this greasy bird's, but he had to admit that he had spoken what looked very like a mouthful. He said he believed that Jas Waterbury had got something there, and Jas Waterbury said he was convinced of it.

'You get two blokes that's rivals in love,' he went on, elaborating his point, 'and another bloke comes along and makes monkeys out of both of 'em, and what happens? It draws them together. They're so sore on the other bloke that they forget their little tiff. That's human nature.'

In a cooler moment Oofy would probably have pointed out that the snag about that was that Porky Jupp and Plug Bosher weren't human, but he was too stirred to think of that now. He slapped Jas Waterbury on the back and said he was a genius, and Jas Waterbury said he had been from a child.

Then Oofy's joyous enthusiasm started to sag a bit. The thought that had sprung into his mind had been that here was a job right up Freddie Widgeon's street, Freddie being the sort of chap who can make love to anything. But he couldn't approach Freddie. And, failing Freddie, who could handle the assignment? You couldn't just go to anyone and ask him to sit in. It would mean tedious explaining, and of course, one didn't want to let the whole world into the secrets of professional wrestling.

He put this to Jas Waterbury, who seemed surprised.

'I was thinking of you,' he said.

'Me?'

'That's right.'

Oofy goggled.

'You expect me to make love to that—'

He paused, and Jas Waterbury in a rather cold voice said, 'That what?' Oofy, loath to wound an uncle's feelings, substituted the word 'girl' for the 'gargoyle' which he had been about to employ, and Jas Waterbury said that it seemed the only way.

'You want to protect your investment, don't you? You don't want all that lovely splosh to slip through your hands, do you? Well, then.'

He had struck the right note. The last thing in the world Oofy wanted was to lose any lovely splosh. It was true that the last thing but one was to make advances to Myrtle Cootes, but, as his colleague had pointed out, it was the only way.

'Right ho,' he said in a low voice, like a premier basso with tonsillitis. 'How do I start?'

'Take her for a nice little spin in your car,' suggested Jas Waterbury.

So Myrtle Cootes was summoned and told to put on her hat, coat and scent, and Oofy took her out for a nice little spin in his car.

When he returned, a good deal shaken and breathing rather heavily through the nostrils, Jas Waterbury informed him that the treatment had begun to work already. The green-eyed monster, running up their legs and biting them, had caused Porky Jupp and Plug Bosher to watch the expedition set out with smouldering eyes and grinding teeth; and scarcely had Myrtle Cootes's patchouli faded away on the evening breeze before they were speaking to each other for the first time in days and, what is more, speaking in a friendly and cordial spirit.

The spirit of their conversation, as Jas Waterbury had predicted that it would be, was Oofy and the many things they found in him to dislike. Porky had criticized his pimples, Plug his little side-whiskers, and each had agreed unreservedly with the other's findings. On several occasions Plug had said that Porky had taken the very words out of his mouth, and when Plug described Oofy as a la-di-da Gawd-help-us, Porky said Plug put these things so well. It had been a treat, Jas Waterbury asserted, to listen to them.

'It looks to me,' he said, 'as though the rift and breach was pretty near healed. Twice I heard Plug call Porky "cully", and there was an affectionate look in Porky's eye when Plug said you reminded him of a licentious clubman in the films which it would have done you good to see. I helped the thing along by telling them that you'd been hanging around Myrtle for weeks, bringing her bouquets and taking her to the pictures, so one more push, cocky, and we're home. What you do now is kiss her.'

Oofy rocked on his base.

'Kiss her?'

'It's the strategic move.'

'But, dash it—'

'Come, come, come,' said Jas Waterbury reprovingly, 'you don't want to spoil the ship for a ha'p'orth of tar. Think of that crowded hall at Huddersfield,' he urged, for it was in that thriving town that they were billed to open. 'Think of those rows and rows of seats, crammed to bursting. Think of the splosh that'll have been handed in at the box office to pay for those seats. Run your eye over the standees at the back. And when you've done that, think of the return match and the rubber match and all the other matches at Leeds, Wigan, Middlesbrough, Sheffield, Sunderland, Newcastle, Hull and what not.'

Oofy shut his eyes and did so. The result was immediate. He ceased to hesitate, and got the do-or-die spirit. It was true that many of the seats alluded to would be merely shilling ones, but Jas Waterbury had spoken freely of a ten-bob top and once you start thinking in tens the total soon mounts up. When he opened his eyes again, there was a gleam of courage and resolution in them. A faint feeling lingered that he would much rather go over Niagara Falls in a barrel than kiss Myrtle Cootes, but nobody was asking him to go over Niagara Falls in a barrel.

'She'll be bringing in the dinner in a minute,' said Jas Waterbury. 'If you look slippy, you can catch her in the passage.'

So Oofy looked slippy and caught Myrtle Cootes in the passage. As his eyes fell on that ginger hair and that fishlike face, there swept over him once more a feeling of regret that Freddie Widgeon was not available. There is probably not a girl in the world, not even Myrtle Cootes, whom Freddie couldn't kiss with relish. It seemed hard that with a specialist like that to hand, he couldn't utilize his services. Then he thought of Freddie's ten per cent commish, and was strong again.

Myrtle Cootes was looking so like her uncle, that kissing her was practically tantamount to kissing Jas Waterbury, but Oofy had at it. Shutting his eyes, for he felt happier that way, he commended his soul to God and folded her in a close embrace. And scarcely had he done so when the air was rent by a couple of hoarse cries and a massive hand descended on his right shoulder. At the same moment another, equally massive, descended on his left shoulder, and he opened his eyes to find the two gorillas regarding him with all the aversion which good men feel towards licentious members of clubs.

His heart did three somersaults and dashed itself against his front teeth. He had not foreseen this angle.

'Coo!' said Porky Jupp.

'Cor!' said Plug Bosher.

They both then said, 'Lor-love-a-duck!'

'Ho!' said Porky. 'Making her the plaything of an idle hour, are you? Well, stand still while we break you in half.'

'Into little pieces,' said Plug Bosher.

'Into little pieces,' said Porky Jupp, accepting his friend's suggestion. 'When we've done with you, your mother won't know you.'

Oofy, contriving to disentangle his heart from his front teeth, said he didn't have a mother, and the two gorillas said that that was immaterial. What they had meant was, supposing for the purpose of argument Oofy had had a mother, that mother wouldn't know him, and the conversation was threatening to get a bit abstruse, when Jas Waterbury took the floor.

'Boys, boys,' he said soothingly, 'you've got the wrong slant. You misjudge Mr Prosser. There's no harm in a gentleman cuddling the lady he's engaged to be married to, is there?'

Porky Jupp looked at Plug Bosher. His eyes were so small that you could hardly see them, but Oofy could spot the agony. Plug Bosher looked back at Porky Jupp and it was plain that if he had had a forehead, it would have been seamed with lines of anguish.

'Coo!' said Porky. 'Is that straight?'

'Cor!' said Plug. 'Is it?'

'Certainly,' said Jas Waterbury. 'That's right, isn't it, Mr Prosser?'

Oofy, who from the very inception of these proceedings had started to turn a pretty green, hastened to say that Jas Waterbury was perfectly correct. He had never liked the man, but he was conscious now of a positive reverence for his sterling qualities. A fellow who thought on his feet in an emergency and said the right thing. I believe if Jas Waterbury had tried to touch Oofy for half a crown at that moment, Oofy would have disgorged without a murmur.

At this point Myrtle Cootes announced dinner, and they all pushed in.

Dinner was a silent meal. It always checks the flow of small talk if fifty per cent of the company have broken hearts, and it was plain that those of Porky Jupp and Plug Bosher were smashed into hash. When they wiped their gravy up with bread, they did it dully, and there was a listlessness in the way they chivvied bits of roly-poly pudding about the plate with their fingers which told its own story. At the conclusion of the meal they went sadly off to the garden, Jas Waterbury following, no doubt to comfort and console. Oofy remained where he was, smoking a dazed cigarette and feeling like Daniel after he had shaken off the lions and had a moment to himself.

Still, though he had passed through the furnace and would have to absorb at least a quart of champagne before he could really be himself again, he was happy. Porky Jupp and Plug Bosher were reconciled, and would give of their best before the discriminating residents of Huddersfield, and that was all that mattered. He took out his pencil and paper, and started to work out the probable takings, assuming that at least the first six rows were ten-bobbers.

He was still at this task when Jas Waterbury returned. And the greasy bird's first words sent a black frost buzzing through his garden of dreams.

'Cocky,' said Jas Waterbury briefly, with no attempt to break the bad news, 'we're sunk. Everything's off.'

'Whark?' cried Oofy. He meant to say 'What?' but in the agitation of the moment he had swallowed his cigarette, and this prevented bell-like clarity.

'Off,' repeated Jas Waterbury. 'O-r-ruddy-double-f. The thing's gone and worked out all wrong.'

'What do you mean? They're like a couple of brothers.'

'Ah,' said Jas Waterbury, 'but they've decided to chuck wrestling and go out to Africa together, where might is right and the strong man comes into his own. They say that after what's happened, they just wouldn't have the heart to wrestle. What's that word that begins with a Z?'

'What word that begins with a Z?'

'That's what I'm asking you. I've got it. Zest. They say the zest has gone. Porky says he never wants to be hit on the nose again, and Plug says the idea of having anyone jump on his stomach simply revolts him. Purged in the holocaust of a mighty love, they're going to wander out into the African sunset and become finer, deeper men. So there it is, cocky. Too bad, too bad.'

They sat in silence for a while. Oofy, thinking of that tenner he had given Freddie, writhed like an electric fan, but from the look on his face it seemed that Jas Waterbury had spotted some sort of silver lining. A moment later he told Oofy what this was.

'Well, there's one good thing come out of it all,' he said. 'It's nice to think that Myrtle's going to be happy. I could wish her no better husband. You must start calling me "Uncle James",' said Jas Waterbury, with a kindly smile.

Oofy stared at him.

'You don't seriously imagine I'm going to marry your blasted niece?'

'I haven't got a blasted niece. I've got three nieces who are all good, sweet girls and the apple of my eye, and the applest of the lot is Myrtle. Aren't you going to marry her?'

'I wouldn't marry her with a barge pole.'

'What, not after announcing the betrothal before witnesses?' Jas Westbury pursed his lips. 'Haven't you ever heard of breach of promise? And there's another thing,' he went on. 'I don't know how the boys are going to take this, I tell you straight I don't. They won't like it. I'm afraid they'll want to start breaking you into little pieces again. Still, we can settle the point by having them in and asking them. Boys,' he called, going to the window, 'just come here a minute, will you, boys?'

It took Oofy perhaps thirty seconds to find a formula. He looked Jas Waterbury in the eye and said:

'How much?'

'How much?' Jas Waterbury seemed puzzled. Then his face cleared. 'Ah, now I get you. You mean you want to break the engagement, and you feel it's your duty as a gentleman to see that Myrtle gets her bit of heart-balm. Well, that would be one way of doing it, of course. It'ud have to be something pretty big, because there's her despair and desolation to be considered. She'll cry buckets.'

'How much?'

'I'd put it at a thousand quid.'

'A thousand quid!'

'Two thousand,' said Jas Waterbury, correcting himself.

'Right,' said Oofy. 'I'll give you a cheque.'

You may think it strange that a chap like Oofy, who loves money more than his right eye, should have acquiesced so readily in the suggestion that he pay out two thousand of the best and brightest. You are feeling, possibly, that this part of my story does not ring true. But you must remember that the two pluguglies were even now entering the room, each with small, glittering eyes, hands like hams and muscles like iron bands. Besides, a thought had floated into his mind like drifting thistledown.

This thought was that he could nip back to London in his car tonight and be at the bank first thing next morning, stopping the cheque. By these means all unpleasantness could be averted. The loss of the twopenny stamp he was prepared to accept in view of the urgency of the crisis.

So he wrote out the cheque, and Jas Waterbury, who had asked him to make it open, trousered it.

'Well, boys,' he said, 'all I wanted to tell you was that I'll have to leave you tonight. I've a little business to do in town.'

'Me, too,' said Oofy. 'I might as well be starting now. Good-night, everybody, good-night, good-night.'

Jas Waterbury was regarding him with incredulous amazement.

'Here, half a mo'. You're going back to London?'

'Yes.'

'Tonight?'

'Yes.'

'But how about Myrtle's birthday? Have you forgotten it's tomorrow? You can't possibly leave tonight, cocky. She's been looking forward for weeks to having you kiss her in the morning and give her the diamond sunburst or whatever it is you're giving her.'

Oofy slapped his forehead.

'I clean forgot the diamond sunburst. I must be in London first thing tomorrow, to buy it.'

'I could get it for you.'

'No. I want to choose it myself.'

'I see a way out,' said Jas Waterbury. 'Give her a posy of wild flowers instead. After all, it's the spirit behind the gift that counts. Plug and Porky will help you gather them. Eh, boys?'

The two gorillas said they would.

'He's simply got to be here for Myrtle's birthday, hasn't he, boys?'

'R', said the two gorillas.

'You mustn't let him leave, boys.'

They both said they wouldn't, and they didn't. When Jas Waterbury got up to go, saying that he would have to hurry or he would miss his train, Oofy tried to accompany him and make a quick dash for the two-seater; but those massive hands descended on his shoulders again and he fell bonelessly back into his chair. And Jas made a clean getaway.

It was about a week later that Freddie Widgeon, leaving the club, found Jas Waterbury on the steps and was stunned by the spectacle he presented. From head to foot the fellow was pure What The Well Dressed Man Is Wearing. His shoes glittered in the sunshine like yellow diamonds, and the hat alone couldn't have set him back much less than thirty bob. He explained that he had been fortunate in his investments of late, and what he wanted to see Freddie about was being put up for the Drones. He liked the place, he said, what he had seen of it, and would willingly become a member.

He was just saying that he would leave all the arrangements in Freddie's hands, when Oofy came out of the door. And at the sight of Jas Waterbury there escaped his lips so animal a snarl that Freddie says that if you had shut your eyes you might have supposed yourself in the Large Cats house at the Zoo at feeding time. The next moment he had hurled himself at the greasy bird and was trying to pull his head off at the roots.

Well, Freddie isn't particularly fond of Jas Waterbury and would be the first to applaud if he stepped on a banana skin and sprained his ankle, but a human life is a human life. He detached Oofy's clutching fingers from the blighter's throat, and Oofy, after having a shot at kicking Jas Waterbury on the shin, went reeling down the street and was lost to view.

Jas Waterbury recovered his hat, which had been knocked off in a sou'-sou'-westerly direction, and straightened out the kinks. He put a hand to his head, and seemed surprised that it was still there.

'Coo!' he said. 'That was a close call. My whole past life flashed before me.'

'Tough luck,' said Freddie sympathetically. 'That must have been rotten.'

Jas Waterbury brooded for a moment. He seemed to be thinking something out.

'So you've gone and saved my life *again*, cocky,' he said at length. 'Do you realize that if we were in China you would have to hand over all your property to me, give me all you've got, if you take my meaning?'

'Would I?'

'You certainly would. That's the law in China, when you save a man's life.'

'What asses these Chinese are!'

'Not at all,' said Jas Waterbury warmly. 'I call it a very good rule. You can't expect to go about saving people's lives and not suffer for it. However, I won't be hard on you. Let's call it a tenner.'

'Right,' said Freddie. 'After all, *noblesse oblige*, doesn't it?'

'You betcher,' said Jas Waterbury.

'Absolutely,' said Freddie.

TITLES IN THE COLLECTOR'S WODEHOUSE